BROKEN IN BY THE MAN OF THE HOUSE

TEN UNTOUCHED PRINCESSES WHO GET WHAT HE WANTS

CANDY QUINN CHARLOTTE STORM
ZOE MORRISON KIMMY WELSH
ELIZA DEGAULLE SAFFRON SANDS
LENORE LOVE CECILIA LAWRENCE
STEPH BROTHERS PHILLIPA SAINT

SHAMELESS BOOK PRESS

Paperback/Hardback: All rights reserved. No part of this publication may be reproduced, stored in or introduced into a retrieval system or transmitted, in any form, or by any means (electronic, mechanical, photocopying, recording or otherwise) without the prior written permission of the publisher. Any person who does any unauthorized act in relation to this publication may be liable to criminal prosecution and civil claims for damages.
ebook: eBook versions are licensed for your personal enjoyment only. eBook may not be re-sold or given away to other people. If you would like to share this book with another person, please purchase an additional copy for each recipient. If you're reading this book and did not purchase it, or it was not purchased for your use only, then please purchase your own copy.

Thank you for respecting the hard work of the author.

Copyright 2019 Shameless Book Press

DISCLAIMER

All characters and events are entirely fictional and any resemblances to persons living or dead and circumstances are purely coincidental. All sex acts depicted occur between characters 18 years or older.

CONTENTS

About Shameless Book Deals   v

1. Wanted by the Man of the House by Candy Quinn   1
2. Hunted for my First Time by Cecilia Lawrence   19
3. Brat Behavior by Charlotte Storm   39
4. Last Chance at the Man of the House by Eliza DeGaulle   62
5. Plant it in my Garden, Daddy by Kimmy Welsh   84
6. For my own Good by Zoe Morrison   101
7. Cream for Carmen by Lenore Love   116
8. What Laurie Deserves by Phillipa Saint   136
9. Kevin's Kisses by Saffron Sands   158
10. In His Bad Books by Steph Brothers   175
    Shameless Book Deals   198
    More from Shameless Book Press   199

ABOUT SHAMELESS BOOK DEALS

Get Free Erotica Downloads at Shameless Book Deals

Shameless Book Deals is a website that shamelessly brings you the very best erotica at the best prices from the best authors. Sign up to our newsletter to receive the following benefits from an erotica recommendation service with a difference:

Highly Specific Recommendations: Our system has been put together from the ground up so as to not lump all erotica under a single umbrella. While the service is gathering speed, a combined recommendation service is necessary, but as time goes on, our recommendations will get more specific based on erotica sub-genres, or kinks if you prefer. You choose the erotica sub-genres you want. We are the first to do this on such a scale.

Discreet: Although we are shameless we are also discreet. Our emails go straight to your inbox and our email subject lines will not be overly crass or vulgar. Graphics in our emails will be almost entirely book covers, more closely vetted than the eBook retailers are able to achieve. That said, the emails will be filled with erotica recommendations, so don't gather your friends and family around the computer when you read them if you don't want everybody to know what blows your hair back.

Professional: Shameless Book Deals is run by Scarlett Skyes, a #1 erotica author with an eye for quality erotica.

Quality: All authors/publishers are expected to hold to a high standard for their work and the deals they are offering to our subscribers. Check the Newsletter Submission Guidelines and report any authors that you believe have breached these guidelines. We recognize that not all complaints will be valid, but authors/publishers who are repeat offenders will be blacklisted to maintain the quality of our service.

Free Stories: Every subscriber gets access to a selection of FREE, and in some cases exclusive, erotica. Downloadable directly from our website.

WANTED BY THE MAN OF THE HOUSE BY CANDY QUINN

She doesn't want to have to tell the man of the house the bad news: she didn't get into college. She gets dressed up in her cutest skirt and blouse, with high heels and thigh high stockings, trying to soften the blow. Fortunately for her, there's nothing soft about him when he sees her!

My step-father was working out, topless as usual. His broad shoulders hefting a set of weights up over his head that I couldn't fathom budging. I couldn't help but admire how his body was just… the peak of excellence. Thick, bulging muscles, rippling with each and every motion of his body. Forearms thicker than most men's biceps, to say the least. And a chest that was stony with bulging pecs and abs.

He was always the best of the best at everything he did. And never let me down, even though it's only been us lately, with nobody to help him.

But now I had to give him the bad news.

I was rejected from all the colleges I applied to.

I know I should've gone for some 'safe' schools, but I couldn't fathom the idea of letting him down and going to anything but one of the best of the best. Now I had to give him the news I wouldn't be going anywhere or doing anything.

I was frozen in place, feeling so... unremarkable.

Here I was, watching the handsomest, hunkiest, most successful man I've ever met, further hone and perfect himself, and I had to tell him I couldn't even get into college.

I felt a shiver of fear run down my spine. Though, perhaps it wasn't all fear. Because I can't deny it: seeing him like that, glistening with sweat, bulging with effort from lifting, grunting almost erotically? God, it did a number on me.

I'm pretty enough I guess, but I always felt a little too ordinary. I never got to be the best at anything, no matter how hard I tried. But he never made me feel that way. I got to be daddy's all-star, no matter what I came home with.

Not this time, though.

I fidgeted, fussing with the edge of my pleated skirt. I'd tried to get myself dolled up nice and cute, to soften the blow. He always loved when I dressed up in skirts, blouses, thigh-highs and heels, and I knew that was the recipe for today too. I was about to disappoint him so much, I had to at least look like his adorable daughter for it.

But could I tell him? I waivered, my stomach filled with butterflies and shame. I was about to turn and go when he put down his weights with a metallic clang and looked over at me.

"Hey sweetie, how's my favourite girl?" he asked, a wide smile on his broad face, a well-groomed beard only enhancing his older, daddy-licious good looks. He plucked up a towel and began to wipe himself down a bit, patting his shoulders, his abs. "And don't you just look yummy today," he said, standing up, his chest heaving from his exertion.

I couldn't help but laugh, but it came out as just a little huff of air, doubt filling every particle. I smacked by lip-glossed lips together as I took a tentative step forward.

"It's just my school outfit," I reminded him, but I was pleased at the compliment. My pussy definitely was, because I felt it pulse with delight. I squeezed my thighs together in protest. Now was not the time to get distracted by sinful thoughts.

"I didn't mean to interrupt your workout, though," I said, my gaze trailing over his chest before falling bashfully to the weights on the floor.

"You're never an interruption," he said, reaching out, placing his giant mitt of a hand on my cheek and gently guiding my gaze back up towards him and his warm, smiling face. "Everything else is a distraction from the most important thing in my life: my sweet lil' girl," he said, leaning down from his towering height and placing a kiss on my forehead.

I wished I could just hold onto that moment forever. It was so gentle and tender, and I swear, for a moment, it felt like all my troubles had just disappeared. I could never get over how good he was able to make me feel with the simplest of things, but he just had a way with me.

It was good and bad, that.

Good, because he made me feel warm and gooey like a cinnamon roll every day of my life.

Bad, because he made my pussy warm and wet, and I often had to rush to my room to rub myself, or else face the entire day frustrated and horny.

And having thoughts about your father, a man so much older than you?

That was definitely not a good thing.

"You say that now," I replied a bit bitterly as the magic of the moment faded, and I remembered just what I had to tell him. I knew that he'd give me a look of disappointment. He never had before, but I could picture it on his face, and it stung my heart.

His thumb caressed my cheek and along my jawline, before coming to tease along the edge of my lower lip. His face had such a loving smile on it, and he looked at me with a sparkle in his eyes.

"I'm really gonna miss having you here with me when you go away to school," he said, his voice so deep and husky, not only full of love but... edged with that sexy, rough masculine sound. "You know, I always just wanted you to myself. I'd have homeschooled you too if I didn't have to work," he said with a playful wink at the end.

"Maybe I would have been better off," I said softly, my words barely audible, my eyes hidden from my long, dark lashes. I couldn't stand to look at him right then. I felt like I should have written him a letter and stayed at a friend's house for a few days so I wouldn't have to face him.

I took a deep breath, trying to center myself, but there was no point. Tears sprung to my eyes and my lower lip trembled.

"'Cause, Daddy... I didn't get into school. None of them would have me."

His hand froze, and so did my heart. I shouldn't have told him like this. At that moment I wished anything but to be there, feeling his disappointment. A split-second felt like an eternity!

"Oh sweetie," he said, and those big, thick arms just wrapped around me, his one hand caressing along my spine, on down to the end of my tailbone. "You gotta stay here with me then," he said, kissing my forehead, then my cheek. "Take a year, I'll take time off work... just the two of us," he said, kissing me again, this time practically upon my lips!

He still smelled of good, clean sweat, and his body was a little dewy from his workout, but I didn't shy away. Not even a little. I just lost myself in his arms, in his little, reassuring kisses as I stared up at him with sparkling eyes. My vision was blurred with tears, but I didn't want to let go of him for even a second to brush them away.

"I failed you, though," I sobbed, my heart thudding so hard in my chest I could barely even hear my own words.

His brows furrowed for a second, and he looked confused as he held me, my body so tiny against his towering mass of muscle.

"No, you didn't," he said, that smile returning. "In fact, I'm overjoyed! I'm gonna plan a series of trips with you, right away. We're gonna go all around the world together. Staying at the best resorts, the finest hotels. Eating at the most exquisite restaurants. Just me and my beautiful, special girl," he said, caressing my cheek again then leaning in slowly, placing a lingering kiss upon the corner of my lips. "What do you say, baby girl?" he asked me in a low, soft husk.

I cursed the way my clit throbbed against my white, cotton panties, and I had to squeeze my thighs together again to try to distract myself. It was certainly not the time to be thinking about the way his skin felt on mine.

I'd never have a man who could ever live up to my daddy.

I'd never deserve a man like him.

I've never even had a boyfriend, not even an awkward and gawky one, let alone someone with strength and charm and pecs harder than rocks.

"But why would you do that after I... after I..." I choked up, unable to finish my sentence.

"Because I love you, sweetie," he said to me with so much patience and adoration, his big strong hands caressing my back, my side, lifting my blouse just enough so that his fingers touched my creamy white skin bare. "I know you're upset about this, but… honestly? I know it's selfish of me, but I'm happy. At least one more year with you," he said, then kissed me again. And he tried to make it seem so chaste, but…

I felt the swell of his manhood through his workout shorts, and it pressed against me.

"The thought of you going away for college has been my nightmare for a while now, trust me," he said.

My breath held as my mind raced.

I doubted myself. I must be wrong. I must have been… hallucinating. A very real, hard, throbbing hallucination. It must be all the stress that brought it on. There was no way he could actually be… aroused. Not right then, not after what I told him.

As if in protest of my thoughts, though, I felt him throb again, and my pussy responded in kind. I touched my fingers to his hip, feeling along the Adonis' belt, pushing myself back just a little. But then, I couldn't help it. I looked down, my eyes widening as his cock twitched again!

"You're my perfect girl," he said to me as I stared at the lewd sight of his cock bulging out his workout shorts. "And god you look so good," he said, leaning in, kissing my forehead, taking a moment to smell my hair as he stroked his hand along it. "C'mon. Stay with me, I'll treat you like a princess. And you'll probably learn more than a year of college ever could show you anyhow," he said, kissing down to my ear, almost suckling the lobe. "I want you all to myself," he husked with a throb of his cock.

I'd looked up some dirty movies, but I always felt too embarrassed to really watch them. I used to turn them off almost immediately, shame burning my flesh as I caught a fleeting glimpse of someone's naked body.

But in that moment, I wanted nothing more to go just a little further.

To see him undressed, so that I could fantasize about it for the rest of my days.

He kissed my ear again, and a small little moan escaped my lips, and I couldn't hide the fact that my nipples were stiff beneath my lacy bra and sheer blouse. It suddenly felt very scandalous, and a part of me said I should run to my room and hide.

My pussy was pleading for me to stay, though. Or, at the very least, to touch myself and relieve a little tension. I tried to resist, but my thighs were pressed together so hard that my knees were beginning to wobble.

"You want me to yourself?" I whispered.

"Yeah," he said deeply, without hesitation. "All to myself," he reiterated, his hand caressing my spine dipping lower... too low, because his palm was rounding the bubbly swell of my ass, cupping it. Then squeezing.

"You're still my little girl, but you're a woman... so I can't make you, but..." he bent my head to the side just slightly, bearing my neck to his mouth where he kissed and nibbled. "Stay with me. You belong in this home. Or on some sunny beach beside me, laid out beautifully in a tiny little bathing suit, for all the boys to stare at. But only for me to touch."

His every word just dripped of masculine allure, so rough and deep, it made my body tingle.

I couldn't believe what I was hearing.

It was like I left my worst nightmare and entered into my wildest fantasies. My back arched, pressing my ass into his hand as I bent my neck, letting his kiss me in a way I'd never been kissed before.

And certainly never thought my *father* would be kissing me in such a manner.

So why did it feel so... delicious?

I felt like I was weightless, floating on air, because before I knew it, I felt the wall touch my back. He had me pressed against it as his cock throbbed, his mouth kissed and bit, and his hands, oh his hands…

They roamed over me, caressing, fondling, adoring so much of me. Even going down past my skirt, to my bare thighs above my socks.

"You're such a good girl," he rumbled to me, as one of his hands so brazenly came up to cup a breast through my blouse, feeling its perky, supple flesh through the fabric of my bra and top. "You get me going so much, every time you walk on by in one of your precious skirts, babydoll…" he practically growled those words, and his dick jumped with excitement against me.

"I wore it just for you. Because I thought you'd be mad and if I dressed like your little girl, maybe you wouldn't be so disappointed," I spilled out, confusion and arousal making my brain feel hazy. I stopped clamping my thighs together so hard, the sensation no longer doing anything to calm the furious throbbing of my wet little pussy. I spread my legs for him then, desperate to feel his hands on my body, his touch on my sensitive inner thighs driving me wild.

He took my silent invite without delay, those two powerful hands of his sliding along my thighs, caressing my skin, fondling me as he edged one knee between my legs. He ran his hands up in under my skirt, to my hips where he felt along the edge of my white cotton panties before sliding back to cup my ass cheeks and lift me up, pinned between him and the wall.

"You know me so well in some ways… but not at all in others," he said, kissing my neck again, moving down to my shoulders as he lifted one hand up to begin to slowly unbutton my blouse. "You aren't capable of disappointing me," he said with such certainty. "Just like I know you won't let me down now, when I need you so bad."

My lower lip trembled and I looked up at him as he started undressing me. I couldn't believe it was happening, but with every button he freed, my heart leapt in my chest.

"I don't want to let you down ever," I managed to say, my words still so quiet and uncertain.

My blouse popped open, my perky young breasts almost spilling out of my small bra as he licked his lips and stared at my body, emblazoning it into his head.

"You won't," he reiterated, bringing his hand in to clasp around my breast, fondling it through the cup of my bra as he kissed me, suckling lightly along my neck and shoulder, until all his caresses made my bra strap slip down, and my stiff, pink nipple exposed itself. "You're my girl after all… all mine," he rumbled with desire, his thumb teasing along my areola before his mouth traced down, past my collarbones, to kiss over my tit.

"This is so wrong," I whimpered, unable to hide my arousal, the desire so strong in my throat as I pressed my perky young tit into his mouth desperately. I needed it so bad, and it felt so much better than I could ever have imagined.

His kisses stopped when his mouth found my nipple, and just devoured it. A soft suckling making me gasp and squeal, squirming between him and the wall as my father teased my body like no man had ever come close to doing before. He was brief, popping his lips free soon, but the intensity of it was overwhelming.

"Gorgeous," he said, looking at my glistening teat, then blowing lightly on it, the cool air meeting his warm saliva making me shiver again. "Are you on the pill, sweetie?" he asked me, his voice momentarily more like the father I knew, than the lusty hunk that was ravishing me.

I furrowed my brow, shaking my head. Embarrassment stained my cheeks red, and I couldn't believe he was asking me that.

Especially not after he was sucking on my breast!

I still couldn't believe it was all happening!

"I've never even had a boyfriend, why would I need to be on the pill?"

His face only lit up with an even brighter smile, excitement sparking in his eyes as he brought his hands back down beneath my skirt, fingertips curling into the waistband of my panties.

"See? I told you that you couldn't disappoint me," he said, slowly tugging down my panties an inch or so, before then grasping them tightly. He tore the white, cotton panties in one sharp movement, ripping them off me with his immense strength and leaving my pussy bare and glistening.

"My sweet lil' girl is still a virgin," he said, sounding so very pleased.

"Of course, but... but daddy, this is wrong, isn't it? We shouldn't be doing this," I whimpered, but I prayed to anyone that would listen that he'd ignore my protests. I wanted so badly for him to want me, for him to touch me, for him to be my first.

"I know baby girl," he said to me, caressing my hair again and looking me in the eyes, that fire in his gaze unmistakable. "But daddy needs you... and you're not going to let him down, are you?" he asked me, this time kissing me right on the lips, the brief entanglement too short, as he pulled back, letting his hand slide down his shorts, so that his huge, veiny cock sprang out, throbbing with desire.

My eyes widened, and unlike with the videos, I felt no need to run and shield my eyes.

His cock was... gorgeous. Hard, with huge veins, swollen with desire and it made me even wetter to see it in the flesh.

But then, there was the problem. I never watched far enough in the porn movies to know what to do with it, and I realized instantly that his cock would never fit in my tiny pussy. I could barely get one of my fingers inside myself, and he was much, much, much bigger than that!

My mouth dropped open and I couldn't even remember to answer his question, I was too stunned.

He cupped my cheek again, not changing the direction of my gaze this time, but encouraging me to stare. He kissed the top of my head, his dick pulsating with desire.

"It'll fit, I promise," he said, as if able to read my mind. Though still I doubted him, he was such a towering giant of a man at 6'5, and I was barely 5'1. And the proportions of his cock to my pussy were even more staggering. But when he pressed it in, letting the underside of his shaft rub along my wet slit, the tingles I felt made it hard to dwell on the practicalities of it.

"You like that? The feel of daddy's cock against your little virgin pussy?" he husked into my ear, his own voice dripping with caramel desire.

"Yes," I whimpered, honesty not allowing me to hide my own desires from him. It just felt too good, and I definitely didn't want to displease him. His touch was such a perfect distraction from my worries, and it certainly reassured me that I hadn't disappointed him.

That I wasn't a failure who will always let him down.

He rocked his hips, grinding his cock to my bare slit, until finally he pushes it up along, letting me appreciate just how immense he was. That dick wasn't inside me, but judging by the way it extended up over my stomach and practically between my breasts, it suddenly became hard to imagine it fitting inside me again!

"You won't be a virgin after today, baby… it's time daddy fixed that for you," he said, encouraging me to stare at the lewd site of his humongous gorgeous cock pressed to my body as he kissed my forehead. "And I'm so glad you saved yourself for daddy. It's the only treasure I care about today."

"Will it hurt?" I asked, staring down at the swollen head, a little bit of precum making the tip glisten. I wondered what it tasted like... He felt so good, and his raw, masculine scent was driving me wild, but the sight of his cock pressed against my skin, lifting up my skirt and throbbing against me...

It was unreal, and a jolt of pleasure extended from my clit, making me gasp.

He pulled back his hips, sliding his shaft along my pussy again, then nudging the tip against my pink little folds, letting them flower around his bulbous crown. He kissed my lips, keeping me up and pinned to the wall as my half-exposed breasts rose with my heavy, aroused breathing.

"It'll feel good more than it hurts," he promised me, slowly nudging that thick cock up against my pussy, edging it into me as he stretched that tiny little hole around his shaft with care in his awesome strength. "Mmm... just tell me... if it hurts too much," he grunted out.

"But I'm not on the pill," I reminded him, as if he'd forgotten. As if somehow, he'd just overlooked that he could possibly get me pregnant.

As if the thought of him knocking me up wasn't at once the most sinful and most arousing thought I've ever had in the world. Another jolt of pleasure went through me as his cock began to spear me, stealing my virginity for himself, and I clung to him desperately as the ache started to give way to something sublime.

My warning didn't pause or even slow his penetration, that thick cock sinking into me ever so slowly in the most erotic sight of my life: that tiny little pink flower of my virginal slit straining to its utmost limits, wrapped around my daddy's hard dick and swallowing it up. He only gave a low, gravelly moan at my reminder, and brought a hand up to cup one of my breasts again, squeezing it.

"And you can't go to college if you're pregnant anyways..." he said, his dick throbbing with excitement, straining the limits of my slit so much it made me squeal.

"You want to get me pregnant?" I gasped, and a pleasure of such intensity struck me like nothing else ever had before. It made my mind go blank, like I was nothing but a receptacle for pleasure, and my pussy started to gush honey around my daddy's cock.

His penetration stopped, and I worried for a second he'd realized what we were doing and was about to put an end to it. But when he pulled back, it was only to rock his cock into me again, slowly pumping his hips back and forth as he filled me up with that massive dick of his.

"Yes," he said in a low, throaty growl, his shaft pulsating wildly with desire. "Again, and again, and again..." he rumbled, his shaft edging into me more and more, slowly picking up speed as he filled me up to my capacity and beyond it seemed!

I could feel every throb inside of me, my body so intensely sensitive to every bit of sensation, and I couldn't help but gasp and moan as that pleasure rushed through me again and again. I knew what I was doing was wrong, but I didn't care. I didn't care about anything other than making him happy.

His free hand slid along my thigh, helping me get a tighter grip of my legs around his midsection as best I could. His fingers slid back and sank into my soft yet supple ass cheek as he began to fuck me, truly fuck me. Each thrust made my breasts quake and jiggle as he kissed at my neck, my jaw, my lips... we were actually making love! My daddy and me...

"I'll never let you leave me... even if it means I have to

keep you tied down with a pregnant belly for the rest of my days," he rumbled with desire, his dick throbbing, straining my pussy and making me scream out as his balls swung up and smacked my rear with his ever-growing pace that panged my slit.

Why did the thought of being tied down for his pleasure and amusement make me so turned on?

I truly was sick! Disgusting! A horny, tempestuous teen!

But I didn't care. If that was what my daddy wanted, then that was the little girl he was going to get. I slung my arms around him, kissing his shoulder and collarbone, moaning against his throat.

"You're so big, but it feels so good. It hurts, but in a good way."

My throaty words spilled out amid my pants and moans, and he rewarded me for them, covering my mouth with his, our tongues intertwining as he pounded me against the wall with a rising pace. As big as he was, there's no way my daddy could've fucked me without any hurt, but the flaring of his passions egged him on more, and brought a few more pained squeals and cries from my lips, breaking our kiss.

"Oh god baby, I need you," he rumbled out, squeezing my ass and releasing my breast only to go up and take hold of my neck as he looked me in the eyes. "Fuck, you're daddy's hot lil' angel…" he grunted, his dick pulsating, spurting a bit of pre inside my pussy. "You belong to me… all mine," he growled possessively.

I never thought I'd want someone so possessive and powerful, but he wasn't just anyone. He was the one person in the world who could utterly dominate me and still leave me quaking and begging for more, I was certain of it.

"I want to make you happy," I whimpered desperately. "But this is everything I've ever dreamed of. I was so ashamed…"

His broad, bare chest rippled before my eyes, hard muscles bulging and rolling as he pumped into me again and again, making my much smaller, softer form quake with his lustful thrusts. He moaned and grunted, kissing me, fondling me, groping me all as his cock swelled and throbbed wildly.

"I've never been happier than I am right now, inside of you," he growled out, admitting to his own taboo feelings. "And I plan to be inside of you every day from now on," he said, a shiver passing through his giant form, even making those broad, powerful shoulders quake.

"I want you," I moaned, another quake of pleasure crashing over me, threatening to send me spiraling to the ground if not for his strong hands holding me up and compensating for the trembling that kept going throughout my body.

"I've dreamed of this for so long, even... touched myself, just thinking about you in your own room. I've wanted you so bad, and I felt so dirty, so wrong..."

My every word just excited my daddy further, and his thrusts grew harder, faster, his dick seeming to get even thicker inside me somehow. It was like goading a bull, but I did it anyhow and he gave a low, gravelly moan.

"Fuck baby... daddy's jerked his hard cock to thoughts of fucking you so many times. To thoughts of making you my lil' pregnant wife," he husked, and I saw it in his eyes, his body, every tremble letting me know he was getting close to cumming, even though I knew almost nothing of men or sex. It was just innate. And his cock plowed into me so perfect and deep, hitting something inside me so exquisitely.

"I was probably stroking off my shaft the same time you were rubbing your little slit," he rumbled, loving the thought.

"Oh god," I murmured, melting into his skin, my mouth pressed against the hollow of his throat. "I wish you'd come in, and caught me. Sometimes I thought about that, too.

About what you'd do. Even though... I didn't think you'd ever actually do what I wanted you to in my fantasies."

He held the back of my head and neck, his other hand on my ass as we spoke such sinful confessions. His thrusts grew erratic, his shaft tensing, so molten hot but sturdy as iron as he grunted and moaned.

"You'll never spend a night without your daddy in you and on you again," he promised before he let loose another gasp, and then pounded his exploding cock into me. Repeated thrusts hammering his spurting dick inside me as thick, virile seed shot deep inside my young, fertile depths, again and again and again. That shaft pulsing so many blasts of his cum.

I screamed.

I couldn't help it. It was such an intense sensation, and he was so deep within me that it hurt, but I wanted nothing more than that pain. It was perfect, and even though I knew the risk we were taking, I didn't care. If he wanted to claim me as his and take care of me for the rest of my life, then that was just fine by me.

And if he got me knocked up?

A shiver of delight went through me, thinking about him doting on me and caring for me as I carried his child.

It was so wrong, but in that moment, nothing felt more right than him filling me with his virile seed.

IT WAS the first time he'd emptied his loins into mine, but by no means the last. My big, strong daddy made true on his words, even if they were given in lust.

At first, I still slept in my bedroom, but he came to me every night. And every night caught me playing with myself, only to take over. Usually he'd eat me out first, but he always ended it with another thick, creamy load in my raw, unprotected pussy.

And now, as time to resubmit for colleges approaches, I find myself sunning on a beach. Just like he promised. Wearing a skimpy little expensive bathing suit that showed off my rear and breasts.

And it got my daddy's attention with a leering grin.

"Damn you look so good in that, sweetie," he said, putting an arm around me, hand on my ass as one of the resort workers brought us fresh drinks.

"You sure about that?" I asked, a little self-consciousness setting in as I cradled my round, pregnant belly. It was abundantly obvious to everyone now, long past the point of being able to hide it. Even if I hadn't been wearing a skimpy two-piece.

"You only look hotter than ever now," he said with a grin, leaning in and kissing me deeply, before letting his hand come to rest atop mine on that belly. And I knew he meant it. His libido and lust for me had only intensified since we'd found out I was pregnant with his child... and then again, when I started to show.

"Thanks daddy," I said, unconcerned, since they barely spoke English here, and nobody had any idea we were father and daughter. It was heaven.

"Oh, and just one thing," he said, giving me that serious look and a stern voice, that was all father. It made me shiver. "Don't even think of reapplying to any colleges, sweetie. You're a full-time wife and soon-to-be mom now," he said with a playful wink.

THE END
Get Access to over 20 more FREE Erotica Downloads at Shameless Book Deals

Shameless Book Deals is a website that shamelessly brings you the very best erotica at the best prices from the best authors to your inbox every day. **Sign up to our newsletter** to get access to the daily deals and the Shameless Free Story Archive!

HUNTED FOR MY FIRST TIME BY CECILIA LAWRENCE

Ellie is an inexperienced teen, dangerously following her newly found desires by boldly chasing after her Older Man in the forest. Yet as she enters she realizes how unprotected she truly is when the Green Man, an ancient forest deity takes an interest in her, wrapping her up in generations of rituals her Older Man is involved with. Everything is at stake as Ellie's first time is fought for in the forest.

~

The world was alive and... dirty and... *wriggling* it was too *alive*, this had to be the stupidest decision I ever made. The sun was setting through the tree branches creating a soft golden hue that belied the bustling aggression of all the creatures I knew were beneath my feet and hiding off in the distance.

It wasn't hard to make out the trail, but the fear tugged cold at my chest from the edges and it was all I could do to reassure myself that daddy wouldn't go off the trail unless he felt he had to, that I'd catch up with him soon and it'd be too deep into his solo trek for him to think about turning back. Sure he'd be angry... a little warmth crept into my cheeks and... other places. It was maddening, confusing and *frustrating*, if it weren't for these... *feelings* I could get on with my life but something always pulled me back after my Stepdad Heath. It had been difficult the last year, every interaction with him had become tainted with this... *frustration* and yet knowing he was going to be away for a whole week had driven me wild with need to be with him, to see him, to feel his arms around me again.

While my first steps into the forest had impacted me with the full depth of how wild and primitive this green and untamed land was, it took a few hours for the sinister lack of humanity to really sink in. At any moment I was not with daddy, a bear might happen upon me, a snake might bite me, or worse, even the trees seemed to bend and curl in toward the path and I was alone in the middle of nowhere with no guarantee daddy would even know to try and find me. My body was aching for all the hours of walking and trekking, I worked out and kept myself fit, but this was not something I was used to.

Then what beautiful flowers and idyllic sun-kissed blooms had gripped my attention when I first entered had given way to harsh weeds and thorns, vines and violently brilliant flowers. The flowers were most unsettling of all, I could not help but reach down, drawn to one in particular that stretched up a good foot above the others. It was as if in a dream, extended right to me, the indigo at the outer edges of its petals gave way in the center to reddish pink and finally a deep and intoxicating green stigma. It was unlike anything daddy had brought home for me from his many trips and I couldn't help but feel I was being watched. Yet try as I might to make sense of what was going on, I found my fingers grasping the stiff and thick pedicel and breaking the flower away to wear in my hair. The scent was potent and disarming, a rich earthy cover that gave way increasingly to a masculine musk. I wandered on from that patch along the path and thought on how daddy had brought me back flowers every year and never had he brought these. It was very unsettling. Now more than ever I wanted him, to see him, and the utter lack of his presence on the path had the cold anxiety and terror clawing inward.

The cold of night chewed at me, slowly as the sun disappeared through the tall trees leaving me in a sheer and utter darkness the raw and primal fear of loneliness and vulnerability pulled at the edges of my vision. The light offered by my feeble phone would only last so long. Now the utter stupidity of my decision kicked in and I felt real fear gasping to whimper in terror from my chest. My heart was racing at the heightened certainty of just how fragile my existence was in this place. "Daddy…" I mumbled with numb lips. "Daddy!" The once insistent and enchanting aroma from the flower now became overpowering. "Daddy! Please…" I whimpered, fearing the eyes that loomed in the dark behind me, I could feel them at a great distance but the voice of my daddy was clear in my mind. *Don't look back.* I stumbled and forced my head forward, blinkered, following the trail until I saw him, his tall, broad form, the thick woolen jacket and pack slung over his back his square jaw and rough brown beard hiding a thin smile and dark blue eyes peering out from under his stern brow. I saw it staring past me with a deadly glint, his .357 reflecting moonlight as a cold, unstoppable threat to any and all comers. Then his eyes met mine and they softened, I wanted to cry. I stumbled, the strength leaving my body and he caught me up in his strong arms, where I belonged. And I knew no more.

It was warm and safe. I was in daddy's tent that I knew from summers spent camping in the backyard. "Dad?" I sat up, dizzy with a head full of sawdust and immediately scrambled out of the tent.

"Ellie-" Dad's head whipped about from the dimly lit clearing. My body ached as I crawled over to him and found myself once again in his arms burrowing my head into his chest.

"I'm so sorry I just…"

"Ellie." He said my name, holding me apart from him by my shoulders, his voice was cool and calm accompanying the intense study his pale blue eyes made of me.

"Speak."

And with his word my mind eased from the panic bouts of shame and guilt and collated everything.

"I don't know what's come over me. This time I knew you were leavin' on your important trip but I just… couldn't bear to be apart from you." I spoke softly, the words in part pushing easily off my tongue, but also being drawn out by his eyes in the softness between us out here in the harsh wilderness. "I know… you always said to think first and act later, that I'm always up to some foolish business… but-" and here I caught my breath when I saw his eyes momentarily soften as they had last night. "-but I just had to okay? I stowed away where you usually keep your box of tools under the tarp." His eyes flashed now and I knew he was thinking about the fact that his tools were no longer a day's walk from him in his car. "They're safe in the garage I swear I didn't drop none, no lies daddy." His grip eased on my shoulders and the tension in his body lessened.

"Those are dangerous flowers Ellie, this place is dangerous to be on your own. I know you know that now, but I need you to really *hear me* when I say this so that you remember it even when you're back in the country or the city. This place is dangerous."

"This place is dangerous." I said softly, entranced by his gaze.

"Good girl." He hugged me and I blushed feeling that warmth rise up in my body.

I reached up to feel for the flower I had put behind my ear, suddenly feeling silly for having put it there. But as I felt it I noticed a second one. I tried to pull it away, but they had knit themselves into my blonde hair.

"Don't play with them, they're with you now. I've got to find a way to get you out of here before it becomes a crown."

"A CROWN? Is this part of those strange things you have to do that you never want to talk to me about?"

"Yes. Though I suppose it's too late for that now. You've presented yourself as a bride for the *Green Man*." He eased me into his side, sitting on his thigh like I had done when I was a little girl. I knew now that I was in serious trouble, he hadn't held me like this since poor Jed got run over by a car.

"I'm going to have to tell you some things and you're going to have to listen and then we're going to have to hike. You're going to have to keep pace with me and I'll do my best to answer your questions then." He stroked my back and squeezed me against him.

"My family has lived here for a long time, we have taken many names and many forms, but our responsibility has always been to preside over the lands around the ancient wilderness." With each word he spoke I cast my mind back to the way he had behaved and the way granny had behaved, always looking to broker peace and solve disputes by tact and with as little violence as possible, never leaving a trace. "Every year as part of the bargain for the power to keep the peace out there we were to pay homage to the Green Man of the wilderness, I won't use his true name here as he is hunting us now and I know not what may befall us if we speak it, but suffice to say, we weren't always leaving a bountiful harvest or fatted calf. Esther, your Granny, put a stop to the practice of bringing him young virgins by taking him on herself and brokering a new deal, she was never the same after, but I am thankful for the ease of burden she gave to me." He paused momentarily and sighed letting his hand fall away from my back. "Well, now you've gone and entered the forest during the week of the ancient pact and you're a virgin, and you're bonded to me, and you plucked the flower. You've engaged yourself to him. And rather than simply watch from the shadows, he's hunting us now, hunting you, but I won't leave you be." I was gripped with cool fear once again as I remembered the eyes in my mind, watching me from a great distance.

"Up." He said and I stood immediately.

"Help me break camp, we need to get moving as quickly as possible. You're going to need a lot more breaks than I do during the day, and we have a lot of ground to cover to make sure I pay homage to my ancestors and make the sacrifice and get out of here."

He stood and was quickly about his business. I tried my best to help but felt like a greenhorn fumbling about for the left-handed screwdriver. The intensity of his judgmental gaze and his rough aura was as brutal in absence as it was when present. I struggled to calmly and slowly work through rolling up the sleeping swag and round up the idle utensils daddy had used last night when he ate but seeing them brought to mind that I hadn't eaten.

"You can munch on this while we walk. I hadn't brought enough food for two so I'm going to have to break a few rules, this will have to do for you until then." Without making eye contact, he handed off a pair of granola bars and then finished stowing away the tent into his green rucksack.

"What will he do if he catches me...?" I murmured staring at his muscular form as he hefted the rucksack onto his back.

"Ellie, I'll only say this once. Be very sure when you ask me a question that you want the answer, because I can't rightly keep you from the information. You're still my little girl, but you're an adult now and you need to take responsibility for some of these choices. I'm going to do everything that I can, but if you feel knowing the answers here might stop you sleeping or eating or keeping pace, I need you to exercise judgment because my mind is bent on keeping you safe right now."

I stared at his broad back and imagined him lifting me, carrying me, *kissing me...* I shook my head in annoyance, *why do I keep thinking of that lately?* My knuckles whitened as I chased away the shame and guilt and focused on being the woman daddy needed right now.

"Yes daddy, I feel I need to know. I won't let the information stop me." I said, forcing at my natural gait to keep pace with him on the path.

For a time he walked, seemingly nodding and acknowledging the trees as if seeing old friends. The full breadth of his strange and awe inspiring aura hit me in a wave as I realized the forest itself was bending to *greet* him.

"The Green Man will take you for his bride Ellie, when he touches you, he will claim you and you will be... you will be persuaded by his presence even as his appearance may disgust you. He will dominate you and turn you into a sacrifice for him to enjoy until you become his wife to join the many other wives he has." As Daddy spoke, some of the trees trembled.

"W-where are they? Can't we free them?" I tried really

hard to keep the fear from my voice, to be strong and reliable the way daddy was, but it was so hard.

"They're all around us Ellie, all these trees, all this life, they're all the wives and children of the Green Man." His words were solemn as the footfalls that marked his passage.

His greetings and nods made more sense as I came to see the lives that must have been given to this Green Man by daddy's family over the years. The gravity of what he had said tugged at my stomach, twice now in the breath of a conversation daddy had shared things that made the bile churn in side. *These were... are all VICTIMS like I could be!* I eyed nervously the trees that seemed to sway toward me in curiosity.

"Easy now Ellie, not all are sorry for this state of affairs, the Green Man is a *good* husband as we might understand it. Almost all come to love and care for him in their own way, even today some daughters come willingly to give their love and lives to him. But that is not you, you are not *his*." He finished with a grunt.

Because I'm yours. My mind achingly filled in the missing detail that made all the sickness disappear and left me with a strange warmth in my abdomen.

"Do you know where he is?" I asked trying to move the topic away from my burgeoning feelings." I eyed about again trying to ignore the trees, trying to see between them for movement.

"Well Ellie... normally I know when he's nearby because I'm alone. You see there's a practice among the family that we have learned, and some other folk out there naturally embody this without training, but it's exceptionally rare. But I can tell when there are other things nearby, think of it like ESP but not bullshit. It's like an internal radar, forces ping and I know I'm not alone and I know something is ahead or is following me." He calmly gave these words with little to no care for the speed and gait he strode and I couldn't help but admire how fit he was, how much endurance he had, how powerful he-*Damnit Ellie he's your dad!*

"Wow... but you can't for some reason?" I managed, trying to show I was paying attention.

"Well I could, it only tends to come to me when I attune with nature and purge myself of other human contact for a good many hours. That's how I discovered someone was following me before, I knew it wasn't the Green Man because I looked back with my binoculars and saw a slim figure utterly unprepared for the trek it was on and feared they would call the Green Man, especially given the time and place."

"Oh..." I managed, my face hot with a blush as I imagined daddy watching me in my activewear. Another warm wave of pleasantness rolled through me at the thought.

"Then as I got closer I realized it was you and rushed to make sure you didn't look back and become ensnared. Of course, now that I'm with you, my senses are incredibly dulled. I can only operate off of my experience as a trekker now."

"Is there nothing we could do?"

"Well, if I send you ahead there's all the chance in the world he'll know a path even I don't know that will have him catch you ahead of me." He said ruling out ideas which made me shudder.

"Or we could turn back to safety and hope to slip by him and forgo the traditions of countless generations potentially eternally upsetting the balance of human and wildlife in this part of the world." His voice took a sardonic tone now and I did my best to avoid the guilt and shame I knew would only slow me down.

"Or I could spend eight years teaching you how to cancel out your own energies so that we didn't interfere with one another. Or…" And here he uncharacteristically paused and sighed.

"What is it daddy, please?"

"I don't want to share that option with you unless I have to."

"But what if you do have to?" I asked, my eyes going wide at all the possibilities.

"Ellie, the ancient world operated on very base and primitive trades between forces, blood, tears, and semen. I would have to… ritually make you an extension of myself, and vice-versa in order to counteract your signals. We would need to rut, I would need to claim you and you're my daughter."

I pondered his words, my face completely red now. My breath coming in hard gasps, but I was alive, my blood was pumping and my breasts ached to be touched. " 'Unless you had to-'?" I managed to ask.

"Ellie I'm not letting you go. It's a disgusting thing for a father to do with his daughter. But if I have to choose between that and you being claimed by the Green Man and made into one of his wives, I think we can both agree that sex only has to mean something if you let it here."

"Yes Daddy." I managed to say, trying to keep a stupid smile from my face when I knew I should be mortified.

∽

"He's way too close, he'll be on us by tomorrow at this rate."

"Can I see?" I whispered as I lay next to daddy.

He was hunched over his binoculars as we stopped for another five minute break peering back.

"It depends on the form he is in. If he is in his pure energy form, you'll be shocked into paralysis. But he's unlikely to be in that form if he wants to make speed on us, it takes an entirely different practical incarnation of his being to-" daddy paused and handed me the binoculars.

"At the clearing where we camped last night, just below the rocks." He guided and then I searched.

There. Sliding down the trail from the decline immediately after our camp, ragged, thin, sun-blackened. A scarecrow of a man though tall, he was covered in grime and ash from campfires but the clothes he was wearing were wrong, and it took me a while to realize his clothes were wriggling, writhing vines, that I was seeing a vague understanding of a man, not an actual man and my mind went into shock. That was when he looked directly at me with pale amber eyes the color of the dawn, the color of the dawn for millennia.

"Ellie!" daddy snatched the binoculars from my hands and picked me up.

Even as I was five foot seven and some one hundred and thirty pounds he hefted me as if I was nothing. My eyes were still lost in the pale yellow as daddy swore and rubbed my back, carrying me away.

I was lost. My body moving now completely on instinct, my mind was strangely blank in a sea of the earthy musk that came from the flowers in my hair and I reached up to feel them. There was a ring forming now through my hair. All that kept me in this world was daddy's hand holding mine, pulling me along. There was a drumming in me, a beating, a heat that wouldn't subside. I needed to be touched. I needed to be filled. I need to be *fucked*.

"Daddy... I need-"

"-hush." His voice was assertive and brooked no argument.

Yet as we walked I caught my hands touching myself, rubbing at my breasts, my hard nipples, my pussy, I rubbed my thighs together sighing at the delicious friction. My mind was full of the Green Man, filling me. Taking me. Making me his. I would be another tree, giving birth to many flowers and plants in the woods as he claimed me again and again with his seed. His disgusting wispy form standing over me, rutting into me. Grimy hands pawing at my-

"ELLIE." Daddy was over me, in the tent. My aching pussy sopping wet as I rubbed and masturbated freely.

"Snap out of it!" His words, usually so easy to obey, couldn't reach me in the fog of my mind, they were somewhere out there in the wilderness, but here, all there was was pleasure and the Green Man.

"Fuck me." I breathed. "FUCK ME." I moaned. "FUCK ME PLEASE!" I begged. The growing raucous need had me delirious with the want for his cock right here and right now.

Then he kissed me. The sharp sweetness of the apple cider he had been drinking filled my senses as he leaned into me. I invited his tongue with my own, my moans now mewls as I melted into his intimacy. He caressed my cheeks as he kissed. Hands roaming down to ease my hands away, tenderly manipulating the bliss out of me, he quelled the urgency into a slow burn. My legs parted wider, instinctively giving him access.

"Ellie, you're my girl, my good girl, stay here with me." He whispered, in a pleading tone I had never heard from him before and my chest was full of love for this man.

His muscular form filled my view. He kissed me again, brushing my hair aside and calming me. I loved everything about him. Even as he kissed me, his manhood urgently pressed against my hot center eliciting a growl of need from me. The light from the tent framed him over me and there was a shadow of the Green Man over me. I started, my mind trembling as I considered that this was the Green Man now, taking the guise of my daddy to seduce me. He eased inside and I howled. "DADDY PLEASE!" I shivered. The sharp pain of his intrusion breaking me free momentarily from the vision of the vines crawling in knots across daddy's form, of him unravelling into the Green Man himself.

"Stay with me Ellie." He called and gently pressed deeper.

It seemed that no matter how wet I was, it simply couldn't make my first time painless. He paused for a time, nibbling at my lip, caressing my breast, teasing my nipple as I rode the wave of pain. Then I nodded to him in a silent understanding when I was ready and he eased deeper. I grunted. It was inconceivable how long and wide he was. It seemed he went on forever. The same process. The same tenderness. The same easing. Then he was in me in his entirety. My hands gripped at his shoulders. His breath was hot on my neck. The same pheromones that I used to sleep at night with his old shirts and pillows now flooded my senses and eased my mind. The sheer heat of his skin on mine, the power of his muscular body made me feel so powerless beneath him.

"I love you, stay with me." He said, caressing me with thoughts, with words, with his touch.

The depth of his intimate love filled me even as we parted and then forced the breath from my lips as he went deep again. Now the warm pressure was building, was flooding my senses with that intoxicating fog. I wanted more of him, my fingers grasping at every inch of his skin.

"Oh fuck yeah." I moaned to the new rhythm of his insistent thrusts. "Fuck yeah Daddy." I leaned my head back and let it all out. "FUCK!" An orgasm ripped out of me suddenly and violently. His body mashed against my clit and made me jerk in a convulsion, the warm bliss like an electric jolt running through my system in a rapid wave that lingered satisfyingly. Yet he didn't stop, he didn't even slow. There again was that sensation that the world was not as it was supposed to be. I the shadows were long from the light and it was harder and harder to avoid seeing the writhing vines in his form, in his tongue, the intoxicating oppression of his scent.

"Mine." He growled, thrusting into me now as I clung for dear life.

His thick cock filled my entire world as it filled me. Thrusting again and again driving all the preoccupations of the outside world from my mind. Every inch of my body was being filled with his desire. Soon it was as I was merely a receptacle for his lust, for his seed, for his brood. It was all my mind could think on. *I will be the mother of his child. I will raise his child. I will bear his child. My body will change for him. I will be his.*

"Daddy." I whimpered.

"MINE." He thrust, the thick hot cum flooding from his member into my fertile womb, his cock filling my newly deflowered pussy.

I lay there, panting as his hot, sweaty body covered mine.

∼

THE TRAIL BECAME EASIER NOW. Daddy was a little colder. But we made rapid progress as he found easy paths through the curves, dips and rises that the natural path followed. Sometimes it felt as if we were in a different time or place, entering into tight passages where the trees made way. I could see a halo of green garlands wreathing above daddy sometimes in the dawning light. But I dared not ask him about the deal granny made with the Green Man. Afraid of what I would discover.

At night we would camp for a few hours, rest didn't feel necessary anymore as he fucked me. Each night seemed to fill me with a fresh energy, a reformed biological process overwriting all the inefficiencies that had plagued me before making me keep pace, making me blend in, making me a passenger of the forest. And those nights turned into short breaks on the trail. He would nod to a tree or to a rock wall and I would lean up against it obligingly. His thick cock pulling moans and grunts from me. Our bodies slapping together in the same wild rutting. It soon became that there were no words passed between us. There was a mutual understanding. A shared experience as the crown started to from on my head. I came to know that soon there would be a fight. A fight for me, the right to own me. Perhaps before daddy could have left me there and been about his business, but now he had claimed me and I was supposed to be a sacrifice, a virgin prize for the Green Man.

I was in a lurid dream of ecstasy, floating along the path as we stopped every few minutes to rut. I started to entice him, noticing my slight form had given way to a womanly figure, my ass had become a weight to sway, my breasts had become a bust to entice, to nurture. As we travelled I found new confidence and knowledge in my body.

On the fourth day. I was leading. The many winding paths of the forest became as one to me and I danced ,between them, through them. And I laughed as daddy chased after me, it had been hours since he had left his mark on me, left his seed in me, and he was growing needy. Yet I skipped away from him, letting the sway of my naked hips tease him. Feeling the burning rage of his frustration build to match that of the Green Man I giggled in giddy glee. Then I gasped as he suddenly snared me.

He fell on me, into the grassy undergrowth, his hard cock entering me in a fluid motion. He wrestled with my body, his hands gripping my throat. Pinning me down stealing the breath from me. My mind raced in an urgent need to live even as every signal told me I was dying, all my body was shutting down just to feel the pleasure he was giving me, that he was drawing from me, that he was pushing into me. "YES." I burbled with spittle and mindless abandon as the wet slap of our bodies echoed in a frenetic frenzy. I was so wet for him that there was no possibility to claim innocence I wanted this, I wanted his dominance, I wanted his ownership, I wanted to be his forever here.

Then his grip eased, his seed flooded into me again and I was wrapping my legs around him, moaning in in approval of the gift he gave me. Out here in the witness of every wife and child of the Green Man, was proof of my submission, of my desire, of my true owner. Here, was where the crowning garland of the flowers in my hair now completed and fell about my neck tightly. And in this state I knew I could not refuse him. I could not refuse my father.

"I love you." The first words I'd spoken for two days, in my hoarse voice. And never had I felt anything truer. Here I saw the change in him.

We were in a clearing now above a rise that overlooked a good portion of the forest. The moon gave light to our nascent glory and allowed me to see in our exposed state that he no longer had his pack, his gun, or his clothes, both of us were naked. Here in the sex filled haze of our bodies I could see the cooking fire of the Green man below, not an hour away, but separated by the cliff.

"This was the last offering." Daddy panted, the vines and green aura of his being fading into flesh and blood that made up his perfect physique. "Now we just need to make it back to the truck." With a sigh he closed his eyes and meditated. I came to understand in that moment that we had been the sacrifice this year for the forest, our energy, or bodies had become engines for the primitive sexual desire that brought life and virility back to the forest even as it imbued our souls. Even as it blessed my womb and his seed.

"Even with the wives helping us, we won't make it to the

truck in time. He will catch us on the morrow. I cannot let that happen. But in all honesty Ellie, I did not prepare for any of this, I did not plan for any of this, I never thought this would happen to us, I didn't know what would happen and I've been trying my best to keep things okay, to keep you safe and I've already failed more than I thought I could bear. Now I face the fact that tomorrow I will still lose you, even if it may feel like lifetimes in this forest with you. Tomorrow he will catch us and I don't even have the gun to kill him." He sat with his head in his hands.

I was filled with a sudden calm certainty. I sat up and leaned over him. My breast at his head enticing his lips while my hand wandered down his toned stomach. "Relax. Focus on me." I purred teasing at his rapidly engorging member. I smiled lovingly as he suckled at my newly hefty breast. I wrapped my fingers around his cock still slick with my juices and stroked him eagerly. I couldn't keep my mind from the thought of taking him inside me yet I wanted to taste him.

I stroked him for a time, fast and slow, letting him build and break. Until I couldn't resist anymore and leaned over him, taking his length into my mouth, it was worth it to hear him groan. There was something different about the unbidden human reactions of daddy as he let go, to the wild visceral grunts and growls of daddy as he rutted. His length filled my mouth, uncomfortably breaching the top of my throat in a burning ache that left me gagging momentarily. But I could taste him, I could taste me on him and the feel of his hands on my head, grasping into my hair controlling the way I bobbed on his member. Then he eased me back up to take a breath, the burning discomfort stuck with me, but I panted, taking in his scent from the source. Nursing, sucking at his balls, licking up the length of the cock that had only recently been buried into me up to my womb and I nuzzled at the tip playfully kissing it. "Fuck Ellie, where did you learn this?" I looked back at him with his cock in my mouth. "The wives of the Green Man daddy." Then I took him deep again all the way in until my lips touched his balls and like that he came explosively down my throat. The sensation was thrilling, even as I wanted to breathe, there was something satisfying about taking his load, of knowing that this was mine, that I had earned this, that I wasn't just a receptacle for him, but an active and equal partner.

I stood up, watching as daddy's eyes lidded and closed, his almost pained, urgent expression now quiet and dull with sleep. With that I moved to the Cliffside and found a vine that I knew was waiting for me.

"Here." The wives had whispered to me. "You know what needs to be done." And I did.

I found my way through the trees and the woods, and the underbrush. Through roots, rocks and treacherous footings I glided until I came to the fire.

There he was, dozing, just as Daddy was. I didn't fully understand it, whether he was daddy's father, or whether there was just some bond passed through granny when she was with him, but there was a connection there. I peered at him. The horrible grimy figure now snoring deeply, and the writhing body of vines that was his real form underneath that illusion. Then I spat out the seed I had taken from daddy, onto the leaves in front of him and whispered to all the wives around, and to his sleeping body.

"This, could have been your seed. I could have stolen it. I am no longer a virgin. I am no longer a sacrifice. I am no longer unclaimed and I could rule you with lust and with the very bondage you seek to claim me by. I could steal your seed and I could claim your throne, but I will not and I shall not. This is your kingdom, but I am not your Queen, I am his. You will respect this and we will share our energy with your wives every year. And you will give us the power to keep the peace as always." As I said this I saw the petals on the flowers around my neck changing color into the green and gold colors my daddy loved so much.

I stood up and again came back to the camp with my daddy, laying down in his arms and breathing in his scent.

In the morning, there was no roar, there was not so much as a whimper, the woods were calm and silent and I was tired. I could see that daddy was exhausted too, our bodies paying for the exertions we had undergone for the better part of a week. Yet it seemed something aided us still through the forest as we made it to the truck with little to no fuss near the end of the day. Daddy didn't speak a word of the sudden change in the Green Man's plans, he must have understood something had happened. He looked at me with wonder and awe every now and then and I felt great pride in causing it. It wasn't until we were home again that I worried. *What if he doesn't want me anymore? What if he's disgusted by what happened in the forest?*

"Ellie." As if he could hear my thoughts as we left the truck, still naked. "There is nothing about you I don't love, there is nothing about you I regret and having you in my life has been the greatest decision I ever made. Ellie I am proud of you and I never want to be parted again." He wrapped me in his arms and carried me inside. Across the threshold and straight to our bed.

Perhaps it was worth the collar of flowers that I could not seem to remove. Perhaps the Green Man was not so terrifying after all. Perhaps, I thought as my legs splayed apart and rested over his shoulders as he leaned into me, perhaps it was the greatest decision *I* ever made.

THE END
Get Access to over 20 more FREE Erotica Downloads at Shameless Book Deals

BROKEN IN BY THE MAN OF THE HOUSE

Shameless Book Deals is a website that shamelessly brings you the very best erotica at the best prices from the best authors to your inbox every day. Sign up to our newsletter to get access to the daily deals and the Shameless Free Story Archive!

BRAT BEHAVIOR BY CHARLOTTE STORM

Sometimes bad behavior is a cry for a good spanking. Bratty bad girl Veil Sharpton has had a strained relationship with her mother ever since her mother married the ruggedly handsome millionaire, Enzo. Fed up with Veil's bad behavior, her mother threatens to kick her out the next time she steps out of line. After all, Veil's an adult now.

It's an empty threat, and to prove it, Veil borrows her mother's new car without permission. She never meant to crash it into the neighbor's mailbox. Never meant to truly put her mother's threat to the test. When the man of the house discovers what his brat has done, he offers her a way out of trouble. All it will cost is her pride…and her first time. Brat Behavior is a younger woman, older man of the house, her first-time erotic fantasy guaranteed to make you misbehave.

The pounding of my mother's fist on my bedroom door is loud enough to be heard over the music blasting through my headphones. I yank them off and glare at my locked bedroom door.

"Veil Louisa Sharpton! Open the damn door."

Shit. Mom just middle-named me, which means she's looking for a fight. No civil conversation starts by yelling someone's full name through an inch and a half of wood.

Whatever. If it's a fight she wants, it's a fight she'll get, something I've gotten better at over the past two years. Ever since she married my stepfather, Alonzo. Enzo for short.

Ask anyone who knows me and they'll tell you I used to be a good girl. The perfect daughter. Always respectful. Then Mom met Enzo. It had been just me and her ever since my real father died when I was six. Now, it's me, her, and *him*.

I want to hate him. Life would be so much fucking simpler if I did. But he's just so damn...*rich*. And generous with his money where my mom and I are concerned. And gorgeous as sin, for a man more than twice my age.

Olive skin. Salt and pepper hair. Runner's physique. Large, rugged hands, calloused from the manual labor he insists on doing with his workers.

You'd think a guy who owned one of the largest construction companies on the western seaboard would be too snobby to get his hands dirty. Not Enzo. He insists on spending a few days a month on site. I overheard him tell Mom that he loves the smell of fresh cut lumber. The heat of the midday sun on his back. The effort of lifting sheetrock into place.

The next thing I heard was his effort as he pounded into my mom. It was his hands I couldn't get out of my head when I locked the door to my room and pleasured myself until I wanted to scream like Mom had.

I'd be a damn liar if I said that was the last time I fantasized about my stepdad. I've rubbed more than one out thinking about what his mouth would feel like on my nether lips. How the scruff of his fuck-you o'clock shadow would feel against the smooth skin on my never-been-fucked pink.

There's something about the gruff way he speaks, the stern way he tries to discipline me when he has no damn right, the look in his eyes after I get in trouble and Mom's not looking. It makes my blood heat. My pussy clench. My nights restless.

That look tells me that he wants to bend me over his knee and spank my bare ass. *Fuck*, do I want to let him. But I couldn't do that to my mother, could I? It's wrong. Me wanting the man of the house is wrong, not to mention impossible.

He doesn't see me as anything more than his wife's bratty daughter. I don't see him as anything other than some rich asshole who came between my mother and me.

"Hold your horses, I'm coming," I say to the door, shame flaming my cheeks at the way I blame Enzo for my problems with Mom.

The distance between my mom and I isn't really his fault, no matter how much I want to blame him. Ever since my dad died, Mom has had a hard time being around me. I remind her too much of Dad. Of everything she lost. Over the years, her sorrow has turned into resentment, and that resentment into endless arguments.

That's why I stole her favorite Burberry jacket to use as a rag when I washed my car yesterday. The cherry red Lexus ES350 Enzo bought me for my eighteenth birthday last month. Mom thought it was an inappropriate gift, bitched and whined until Enzo bought her an even more expensive Mercedes.

What was inappropriate was the way she acted like a

child. Also inappropriate was the way I hugged Enzo when he gave me the keys, and the orgasm I had later that night thinking about him taking my virginity in the back seat of the car he just bought for me.

The next bang on my door isn't a knock, it's a kick. The door shakes in the frame, bows at the bottom where Mom kicked it.

"I said I'm coming!" I yell at the closed door, her overreaction a trigger for me to escalate the situation. Maybe one day I'll learn not to be such a brat. That day isn't today.

After I unlock the door, I fling it open, dodge a blow aimed at my face. Okay, in all honesty, she was going to pound on the door, not my face. Right now, that distinction doesn't seem all that important.

"Are you fucking kidding me?" I screech, allowing the full force of my well-practiced angst to echo through the house. If Enzo's home, there's no way he won't hear that. Hell, there's no way he can't hear Mom yelling at me first.

When Mom realizes what she almost did, she freezes. Her eyes go wide, and her lip quivers. For a second, I think she might actually apologize. She feels bad about nearly punching me in the face, but that moment ends when her features contort into rage once again. A look I'm all too familiar with.

She holds up the stained fabric of what was once a very expensive jacket. "How many times do I have to tell you to keep your hands off my shit? To stay out of my room?"

I roll out my shoulders, then lean against the open door, try to look as casual as I can. I know my attitude pisses her off. Yes, I shouldn't goad her or make this worse than it already is. The old me would have begged for forgiveness by now. The old me would've never done this in the first place.

That good girl is long gone.

"I don't know." I throw in a sassy shoulder shrug. "How many times have you told me already?"

"Hundreds," she seethes.

"Maybe twenty more times, then. Or fifty. Not sure. Why don't you keep telling me, and I'll think about listening."

"You ungrateful *bitch!*" Mom takes a step toward me, her fist clenched tightly around her jacket. "After everything I've done for you. Everything I've given you."

"You mean everything *Enzo's* given to *us*," I snap.

She scoffs and tugs on the designer silk tank top I'm wearing. "Don't think I haven't noticed the things he's bought you."

What the hell is that supposed to mean? I'm about to ask, when a deep voice cuts into our argument.

"Everything all right?" Enzo's dark brown eyes land on me first, then flick to my mother.

"Peachy," I answer with more than a hint of fake cheer in my tone.

"No," Mom says over the top of me. "Everything isn't alright." Mom holds up the jacket. "Do you see what *your* stepdaughter did to my new jacket?"

His stepdaughter? What the hell? Why is she trying to push me off on him? I'm her actual blood daughter.

Enzo looks as confused as I feel, but then quickly wipes his features clean, something he's exceptionally good at when it comes to not getting between my mother and I.

He takes the jacket from Mom and inspects it. "Is it true?" he asks me. The hard set of his lips, the stern look that only his eyes convey, make me want to answer truthfully. They also make me want to be a brat.

"I needed something to dry off the new car you bought me for my birthday. I didn't want to leave water spots after I washed it. Honestly, I thought it was a rag."

I swear to fuck Enzo's lips curl into a smile before Mom launches into more yelling.

"That's *it*. I'm sick of your shit. I want you *out* of my house!"

I don't bother keeping the bitter laughter from my voice when I say, "Don't you mean Enzo's house?"

It pisses Mom off that I've never treated anything belonging to Enzo as also belonging to her. Maybe it's because I can see she's using him. That she doesn't actually give a shit about him, just his money. That she spends a lot of time secretly texting on her phone with a yoga instructor she sees way too many times a week to be as uptight as she is.

She snatches the jacket from Enzo and throws it at me. One of the buttons hits next to my eye. A millimeter to the left, I'd be blind. I take a step back, put a hand to my cheek. It doesn't stop my mom.

"I mean it, Veil. Pack your shit and get ou—"

Enzo pushes past my mom, steps into my room, brings his hand to my injured cheek. "Are you okay?" he asks. His gruff voice sends liquid heat down my spine, which pools in the eager, unused, and greedy hole between my legs.

"Are you fucking taking her side?" Mom shrieks.

Enzo ignores her, keeps his smoldering gaze on me until I answer him. I don't do it vocally. No, speech is impossible with his body so close to mine. With the way his expensive cologne coats my tongue.

I nod. It's the best I can do.

"I think you need to chill," Enzo says to Mom, his hand still on my cheek, the heat from his skin more painful than the stupid button. But it's the kind of pain I like. The kind I crave. "Why don't you see about taking a yoga lesson?"

The way Enzo says *yoga lesson* makes me think he knows about Mom's extracurricular pose practice. Is spread eagle a yoga term?

Mom opens her mouth, closes it, then sticks out her lip like a child who didn't get her way. "Fine," she says. "I'd rather do yoga than be here."

"Don't you mean you'd rather do your yoga instructor?" I mutter, but Enzo's standing too close. The way his body tightens and his jaw ticks tells me he heard. I try to feel sorry about that. I don't.

"She's your problem," Mom says to Enzo. "You deal with her." With a final huff and stomp of her foot, Mom takes off down the hall.

When Mom's gone, Enzo releases my cheek. He takes a step back, puts up the wall that's been between us ever since him and Mom got married. "You shouldn't disrespect your mother the way you do," he says, his tone implying I'm the one at fault.

I cross my arms underneath my tits, which pushes them together. They spill out of the top of the tank I'm wearing. "She's a bitch. She shouldn't talk to *me* that way."

His eyes flick to my cleavage, then down to my hips before making a return trip north. Fuck do I want him to explore every ridge of my landscape.

"She may be a bitch, but you're not the one who has to deal with her later."

I tap my foot and move my neck with attitude when I say, "Your problem, not mine."

Enzo's dark eyes flash with something too quick to analyze. The space he'd put between us closes, and he towers over me, not in a threatening way. In a possessive one.

He doesn't lay a hand on me, and honestly, I'm not sure what I'd do if he did. He doesn't need to touch me to get his point across. The heat kicking out from his skin is enough.

"You are such a naughty, bratty girl," he says, tone gruff like it always is. But underneath is a current of something playful. Something primal. "If you were *mine*, I'd take you across my knee."

His? His what?

My voice shakes when I ask, "Y-You mean if I were your daughter?"

"No, Veil. That isn't what I mean."

The chill that replaces his heat when he turns from me and leaves my room is like a bucket of ice water to the face.

"Behave," he says over his shoulder. "Or the next time you step out of line, I'll have to punish you."

I'm not sure why, but something about the way he just said that makes me more reckless than I've ever been. Suddenly, all I want to do is cause trouble. Underage drinking should do the trick. Hell, maybe I can even get arrested.

It isn't long before Enzo retreats to his home office. I can hear his fingers click the keyboard. I wait a few more minutes, then make my way into the kitchen, to the drawer where we keep our keys.

Mine are gone.

I run to the front room, look out the window. My car is there, and so is Mom's. She must've taken my keys, then taken Enzo's car instead of her own. Fine. She wants to take my things? I'll take hers.

After throwing on a light jacket that I took from her closet last week, I grab Mom's key fob and get into her car. It's nice. Nicer than she deserves. I don't know why the hell Enzo didn't just tell her *no* when she threw a fit to get it.

I press the start button and don't bother putting on my seat belt. The more rules I can break, the better. The rearview mirror provides me the reflective surface I need to apply some lipgloss and fix my hair. Sure, I'm eighteen. But if I style myself just right, I can pass for twenty-one.

After I fluff the girls so the right amount of cleavage

shows, I throw the car into reverse. Movement catches my eye. When I glance up, my gaze meets Enzo's.

Seeing him there, arms crossed, stern expression on his face, makes my heart jump into my throat. I'm pretty sure a loud, "Eek!" escapes my mouth. Flustered, I slam on the brakes. Only, that isn't the brake pedal.

The car jumps the opposite curb, and only stops when it hits the neighbor's mailbox.

Shit. Shit. Shit. *Shit!*

Mom's going to kill me. The look on Enzo's face tells me he might do the same. Sure, I meant to get into trouble. But not this kind of trouble. Not the kind I can't sweet talk my way out of.

The driver door whips open. Enzo's scent slams into me harder than I just hit the mailbox. "Are you okay?" he asks.

It takes me a moment to realize he isn't yelling at me. That he's actually concerned.

My fingers tighten on the steering wheel. "Y-Yeah. I think so."

Enzo reaches in, brushes my hair off my forehead. God, his touch. Even now, he's the thing I can't stop thinking about. Not the car. Not the fact that Mom will kick me out after this. It's just *him*, and his perfect fuck-me smirk.

"You aren't going to tell Mom about this, are you?" I ask with more than an edge of panic.

Enzo cocks his head to the side and studies me, like I'm some kind of blueprint he isn't sure how to read. "It depends," he says after what feels like forever.

"Depends on what?" I ask.

I swear he fights a grin when he says, "On how well you beg for my forgiveness."

Begging isn't something I normally do. For him, I'll do it. I'd do anything.

"Please! *Please*, you can't say anything. She'll kill me. Or kick me out. I don't want to go. I'm sorry, okay. I'm sorry. I'll do anything. *Anything*. Whatever you tell me, Enzo, I'll do. Just…please. Help me."

Without a word, Enzo pulls me from the car. He isn't rough in an angry way. No. It's more like when he gives a directive, he expects utter compliance.

He jumps in, pulls the car back into the driveway. I follow on foot, take my sweet ass time. Enzo throws the car into park, closes the door, and stalks toward me.

The man looks like a damn predator. I'm definitely the prey.

After a few steps, he stops and beckons me with his finger. "Come here, Veil."

There's something about the quality of his voice that makes me want to obey. It also makes me want to misbehave even more. See how far I can push him.

My hands find my hips as I throw out a sarcastic, "Or else what?"

Every line of Enzo's body tightens. His back straightens. His jaw muscles ripple, the after effect of my bratty nature splashing around in an otherwise calm pond.

The next time he speaks, I know I have a choice to make. I can either pack my shit and get out, or I can do anything and everything the man of the house tells me.

I choose option B.

"Or else I won't help you. I won't say it again, Veil. Come. Here. *Now*."

My throat goes dry, every drop of moisture wicked away by the raging river between my thighs. Does he know what his voice does to me? Know how many nights I've fallen asleep touching myself with him in mind?

It's wrong. Wanting to fuck my stepdad is wrong. If there's anything I'm good at, it's breaking the rules.

I nod instead of trying to speak—which I can't do right

now, anyway—and get my ass moving. Enzo isn't the type of man you keep waiting. Not if you want to please him.

My heart thunders in time with my footsteps as I make the long march up the driveway to where he stands. I stop when barely a foot separates us, and stare at the ground, at his bare feet.

He must've ran out of the house after me when he heard Mom's car start.

"Good girl," he says so low I almost don't hear him, but I'm standing so close, there's almost no way I can't hear.

He puts his fingers underneath my chin and lifts until my gaze meets his. "Do you remember what I said I'd do the next time you stepped out of line?"

I try and swallow, but there's no way that's happening. "You said you'd pu-punish me."

His grip on my chin tightens. I gasp, in pain, sure. But also because my blood heats and my nerve endings come alive at the way he touches me.

No one's ever touched me like this before. Yes, I'm a virgin, but I'm not a fucking saint. I've been all the way around the bases, but have never scored a run. If it were up to me, I'd let Enzo steal home plate.

His eyes take their time roaming over every inch of me. They take in the stolen jacket from Mom's closet. The tank top he bought for me. The booty shorts Mom always said make me look like a slut.

"As much trouble as you get in, I'd say you like being punished. Do you like to be punished?"

My mouth pops open. My thighs press together. I want to argue his point, but my body wants to agree.

"Yeah, you like it. You're a brat, Veil. A bad girl," he says, eyes smoldering, tone low and commanding. "Do you know what I do to brats?"

I whimper when I shake my head.

"Bratty bad girls get spankings," he says.

If there was a dry patch on my panties before, it's definitely gone now. I close my eyes, lean in to his possessive grip, and probably make some kind of noise that isn't lady-like.

Enzo lets go of my chin and slides his hand around to the back of my neck. For a moment, I think he's going to kiss me, which is stupid. He wouldn't do something like that, would he?

Using his grip on my neck, he turns me until I face the house, then pushes me toward the front door. "Inside. Now."

I trip over my own feet, the flap of my sandal catching on the concrete driveway. He grabs hold of my upper arm to help steady me, then uses said arm to bully me into the house, through the living room, down the hall, and into his private office.

His man cave, he calls it. It's the one room in the house neither my mom nor I am allowed to go. In the center is an imposing desk with *three* computer monitors. I mean, who the hell needs three monitors?

The chair behind the desk is leather and ergonomic. It probably cost him thousands. In the far corner of the room is a couch. The tightly woven industrial fabric is both durable and attractive. Maybe it's soft, too. Can't tell, and I've never touched it.

The cherry wood walls are methodically and artistically arranged with a variety of awards, pictures, and paintings. Enzo's tastes are eclectic. At least, I think the decor embodies what that word means.

Enzo shuts the door, the sound sending a shiver through me. He makes his way to the couch and sits next to the armrest. "Take off your mom's jacket."

I do what he says, let it drop to the floor. His eyes follow it to the ground, then slowly work their way back up to my face. The path of his appraisal sears my exposed flesh. A tank top and booty shorts don't cover much.

"Come." He pats his lap, and it's only then I notice the *huge* bulge in his pants.

Oh, *fuck me*. He's hard, and so much larger than I imagined. Mom's an extra bitch that she cheats on this man. He's rich, smokin' hot, generous, kind to her, and has a large cock. I mean, what the fuck else does she want?

If he were my man, and not my stepdad, I'd worship on my knees every morning, and scream my praises every night. Then again, with the way he's obviously turned on, maybe he can be both.

Doing what he commands, I close the distance between us, turn so I can sit on his lap. "No," he says, not letting me sit. "Not like that. Your knees go here." He points to the couch next to him. "And your chest goes here." He points to the armrest.

That position would put me over his knees, with the couch to hold me up as support. I'd be vulnerable. At his mercy, if mercy is something he has.

Somehow, I manage to do what he says, even though I'm shaking so hard I can barely move. When I get into position, he pushes a lock of hair behind my ear and whispers, "Are you scared to get spanked?"

I shake my head. "Not scared. Nervous. This feels—" I bite my lip. "I'm not sure what you're going to do to me."

His demeanor hardens, something I didn't think possible. "We can stop. We don't have to do this. You can face your mother on your own. Confess what you did. Take her consequences."

"No!" I practically shout, panic making it impossible to stay calm. Not panic about my mother. Panic that he won't spank me. "I don't want to stop. I need this. I'm a bad girl who deserves to be punished. *Please*, Enzo." I draw out the word. "Punish me."

Like a lock clicking into place, something shifts between us. He's no longer just the man my mom married. For the first time in our relationship, he's my *daddy*.

My tits hit the armrest when Enzo pushes me into place. With one hand, he holds the back of my neck, makes sure I'm face down, ass up. With the other, he glides down my shorts, exposes my red lace thong underwear.

"You *are* a naughty girl," he mutters as he pulls my undies down to my knees to join my shorts.

On his way back up, he runs his fingers, featherlight, along my inner thigh. He stops before reaching my slit. He's teasing me, and I hate it. I also love it.

I moan as I press my hips up. At the same time, I lower myself, forcing his hand against my smooth slit. He stills. So do I. I want him to touch, to explore. But maybe he doesn't want to. Maybe I've pushed too far. Maybe this was only ever supposed to be a spanking.

Something like a growl rumbles his chest when he flattens his fingers against me and strokes me from front to back. There's no way he won't be coated in my slick. Also no way he can deny that I wax.

"So. Fucking. *Bad*." His voice is little more than a rumble. A freight train about to derail off tracks designed to make us proper. Inhibited. Ashamed.

I'm not ready when he lands the first blow.

The impact is loud. So am I when I cry out. Iced lava flows from the point of impact, the burning slick filling the space between skin and muscle. The pain both freezes and cauterizes. Both consumes and sets free.

The next time Enzo touches me, he's gentle. His fingertips glide across the area he hit, adding a tickle to the torture. I moan at how good his fingers feel against my flesh, then moan again when he brings them between my thighs.

He pinches my clit. I jump at the same time a shiver tracks its way down my spine. The sensation of him is too much. It's exactly what I've craved since...I don't know when. Maybe forever.

Smack!

The second hit catches me just as off-guard as the first. The delicious heat ignites when he hits me for a third time in the exact same spot.

I collapse against the couch, beg him to stop. "*Ouch!* Fuck. That hurts."

"I know," he grinds out, his breathing as labored as my own. "It's supposed to. You were a bad girl. You forced me to punish you. You made me do this."

He hits me again, this time on the other cheek. I squirm against him, try to get up. But he's too strong. Plus, I'm not sure where I'd go if he did let me up. There's nowhere I'd rather be than right here, in the man of the house's lap, getting spanked.

"I'm sorry, Daddy! I promise I'll be a good girl."

The words roll right off my tongue, smooth as the thousand dollar whiskey Mom hides in her dresser drawer.

"Mmm, I like when you call me *Daddy*."

"Okay," I whisper. I can do that.

"You say you'll be a good girl, huh?" Enzo asks as he trails his fingers down my crack to my swollen lips.

"Yes," I release on a breathy sigh. "I promise."

Enzo moves the hand that had been holding my neck to my mid-back. I still can't move, and it seems that's exactly what he wants.

He teases my folds until they open for him. When he slides a finger inside me, I gasp. "*Fuck*, baby girl. You are soaked, and so very tight."

"For you," I admit. "Only for you."

His finger stills inside me. I wiggle my hips, desperate for some friction.

"Only me?" he questions like he doesn't believe me.

"Yes, Daddy. Only you. I've never…you know, done anything like this. Never let anyone inside like I want to let you inside."

Enzo groans, which ends on my name. "Veil. You're killing me."

Feeling bolder than I ever have, I reach my hand between us, run my palm along the outline of his hard dick. "This only has to hurt one of us." I wiggle my ass so he gets my meaning. "Let me give you some relief."

Enzo bucks his hips up into my hand. I push harder against him, rub in small circles.

He grabs my wrist, removes my hand. I begin to pout when he says, "Don't worry, baby girl. You're going to give me all the relief I require. It's the least you can do for the trouble you've caused. But first, I'm going to make you come for me. Show me what this beautiful pussy of yours is capable of."

Enzo plunges his finger in deep. The hand that had been on my back moves around to my clit. He pinches the small nub, then rubs in circles like I had done to him.

That sensation alone would be enough to make me go off. But then the finger inside me finds a spot that makes fireworks explode behind my eyes. I'm right on the edge of losing it when he pulls out and smacks my ass.

He doesn't hit me as hard as he had before. Hard enough that the pain heightens the intensity of everything else.

Suddenly, his finger is back inside me, working the same internal nub while his other fingers work the external one. He spanks then finger-fucks me, over and over, until I'm on the verge of tears.

"Please, Daddy!" I beg. I don't know what else to do. Every time I think I'm going to come, he pulls out, spanks me, hits the reset button on my orgasm.

"I need to make sure you learn your lesson," he grunts, obviously affected by whatever he's doing to me. "Bratty girls get punished. Good girls get rewarded. What kind of girl are you?"

"Good!" I practically scream. "I want to be good. I'll do whatever Daddy says. Please, I wanna be *so* good. Help me be good, Daddy."

The next time Enzo plunges into me, it's two fingers. The stretch of the size difference burns my opening. But everything else is so euphoric, I don't care. Besides, it's clear I crave a bit of pain with my pleasure.

His fingers curl. He hits my internal node with ruthless precision. I detonate. Every muscle in my stomach clenches. Stars dance across my vision. A primal cry claws its way up my throat, ripping and shredding everything about who I thought I was. Who Enzo is to me.

There's so much warm wet as my greedy cunt clutches at his fingers inside me. I should be embarrassed, because I think I just pissed myself. I'm luckily too blissed out to care in the moment.

"That's it, baby girl. Make that beautiful pussy of yours squirt for me."

Squirting? Is that what's happening? I've heard about it from some of my girlfriends, and the internet, of course. I didn't know I was the kind of girl who could do that.

Seems there's a lot I didn't know that I'm now learning.

When the orgasm finally subsides, my strength gives out. I slump against the couch, let Enzo cradle me in his lap. Not that he gives me any time to rest.

"Oh, no, baby girl. You aren't quitting just yet. Stand."

Somehow, I do, even though my shorts and panties are

around my knees. "Take them off." Enzo juts his chin at my clothes. "Slowly. I wanna watch you strip for me."

I wiggle my hips, let my shorts and panties fall to the floor. Bending over, I unbuckle my sandals, kick those off as well. When I stand, I can't help but notice Enzo looking at me. No. Not looking. Admiring. It makes me want to put on a show.

As slowly as I can, I peel my tank top up over my stomach and tits. For a moment, I'm blind to him as I pull it over my head. I feel him before I see him. His scent, his body heat, both slam into me. Maybe it's because I'm still hypersensitive from the orgasm. Or maybe it's our connection. Doesn't matter.

His lips find mine in the kind of kiss that takes a brat from rags to royalty. I do my best to keep up. But he's so much stronger willed than I am. So much more experienced. If I get the chance, I'm going to beg him to teach me everything he knows.

Enzo's rough, warm hands wrap around me. His fingers snap my bra open, then slide it off. He breaks our kiss and steps back. "You're a fucking knockout, Veil. You always have been. You have no idea how hard it's been to keep my hands off of you for the past two years. I've wanted you in my bed. I've settled for your mother."

His confession sends a heated need through my bloodstream. The car. The clothes. The nice gestures since my eighteenth birthday. They all make sense. He wants me like I want him.

I push my palms against his stomach over his shirt, slide my fingertips down the band of his pants. "I've masturbated to the thought of you more nights than I can count. So, yeah, Daddy. I do know how hard it's been. You don't have to settle anymore."

To make my point, I run both hands over his hard cock.

He growls and kisses me hard before giving me a command I'm all too happy to follow. "Take them off," he says, referring to his pants, as he removes his shirt. "It's past time I take what's mine."

"Yes, Daddy. I'm all yours," I respond as I follow his pants to the floor. His massive cock springs free, bounces a few times in the air. I pounce on it, determined to get the whole damn thing down my throat.

"*Fuck*! Veil." Enzo grabs my hair, whether to pull me off or push me further, I don't think he knows.

I pull out every trick I know. Every trick I've read about, heard about. Granted, I don't know much, but I'm determined to please him. To make him crave me like I crave him.

His toes curl under. His thighs and stomach harden. Good, that means I'm getting to him. Edging him closer to the type of orgasm he gave me.

"Stop. *Fuck*, stop."

Reluctantly, I pop off of him. He tastes amazing, and I want to show him just how much of a bad girl I am. A bad girl willing to let the man of house reform her behavior.

"I thought you said you were a virgin?" he questions as if he doesn't believe me.

"I am a virgin," I insist as I caress my hand over my tits, across my stomach, and stop between my thighs. "I've never let a boy take me here." Not that Enzo's a boy. He's all man. "But that doesn't mean I haven't done this."

Without waiting for permission, I run my mouth along the underbelly of his thick member. The veins pulse and bulge, and a bead of precum awaits me when I reach his head with the tip of my tongue. My reward for making him feel so good.

"Your mouth is magic, baby girl. But I want what no one's claimed. I want what you've been saving for *me*."

Enzo sits on the couch and pulls me toward him.

"Straddle me," he directs. "Facing me. I want to watch you when I take your fresh cunt."

My knees sink into the couch on either side of him. His hand immediately caresses between my thighs. He works my swollen, soaking wet slit. I moan at the sensation. At knowing I'm about to let my mother's husband take my cherry, a fruit I'm more than happy to give to him.

"You're ready for me, aren't you, baby girl?"

I nod and bite my lip, more than a little nervous about how much this is going to hurt. And about what I'm going to ask him.

"A-Aren't you going to get a condom?" I somehow manage to say through the shame burning its way up my throat and into my cheeks. My nerves make it impossible to stay calm, and it's embarrassing having to be the one to bring it up.

Enzo shakes his head. His hair, longer in the front than the sides, sweeps across his forehead with the motion. "No, baby girl. I'm going to ride you bare. I want to feel you, want you to feel me."

"But," I start, embarrassment giving way to panic. "What if I—"

Enzo silences me with a kiss as his hands wrap all the way around my ass and thighs. His fingers find my folds, and he pulls me apart, opens me up so I can receive everything he's about to give.

"Don't worry, Veil. You be a good girl for me, and I'll take care of you from here on out. That's our deal."

By take care of me, I don't know if he means he'll fuck me properly every night, or if he means he'll leave my mother to be with me. Hopefully, it's both.

I don't have time to think about it, or argue the point that I'm too young to get pregnant. That our situation isn't as simple as me trading places with my mom. The fat head of his cock demands entrance. I give it. I give him everything.

When he slides in, the only thing I can focus on is the pain. He's so huge it feels like I'm being split in half. Then he takes my nipple into his mouth, rolls the hard nub around on his tongue. It's just enough pleasure to work through the pain.

I'm vaguely aware of the sensation of being fully sheathed, of my thighs resting on his, of his balls against my ass. "Open your eyes, Veil. I want to watch you take me, and I want you to watch me enjoy you. I know there's pressure. I know it hurts. But it won't hurt for long, baby. Okay?"

The whimper that escapes my lips is pathetic. What happened to the bratty princess who took her mother's car out of spite? She's gone, tamed into submission by the man of the house.

"Okay, Daddy," I say, because there's nothing else to say. He's all the way inside. And I'm all the way his good little girl.

With his hands on my hips, he guides me up and down. He dictates our rhythm until I've loosened enough for it not to hurt. For the pleasure he promised to infect my bloodstream.

"That's it, Veil," he grunts. "Ride me. Show me just how much you've fantasized about this."

I do. It's easy. I've fantasized about being with him so many times, the real-deal so much better than my imagination. I just never thought it would ever be real. That having Enzo like this was possible.

"I'm close," he whispers as he bites my neck, as his hands on my hips make sure I keep pace.

"Me, too," I say, breathless. "Let me know so you can pull out."

"I'm not pulling out, baby girl," he grits out through shut teeth and clenched jaw. "I'm coming inside your tight little pussy. You're gonna take me. All of me. It's your punishment for being a bad girl."

Maybe it's wrong, and more than a little stupid, but hearing him talk to me like that, the thought of him filling me with his seed, sets me off.

My muscles contract around the fullness of him. My nails dig into his shoulders. The warmth that coats my insides isn't only mine. It's him and me mixed together.

A string of curse words leave Enzo's lips as he fucks up into me one last time. His grip on my hips will leave a bruise. I don't care, can't possibly care about anything in this moment. I'm too lost in sensation.

"Fuck, Veil. *Fuck*," Enzo says, over and over, as his cock jumps inside me.

When the pulsing dies down, and I know he's spent, he kisses a trail over my tits and up my neck. "How do you feel?" he finally asks.

I don't answer right away. I'm not sure I can speak.

He slides out of me, pushes us both to standing. His release glides down my inner thighs. I squeeze them together so I don't drip on the floor. "Messy," I finally offer in answer to his question about how I feel. "And deliciously sore."

The kiss Enzo places on my lips is gentle. Maybe even tender. "You were a good girl. I'll take care of your mother's car, tell her it was my fault. I'll protect you. I meant what I said, baby girl. You're mine, now. I take care of what's mine."

He runs his fingers through our combined slick, then over my belly. "No matter what," he emphasizes.

My hand covers his on my stomach, in the place a baby would grow. *Our* baby. "Yes, Daddy," I say, loving the naughty way my nickname for him rolls off my lips. "I'm yours, no matter what."

THE END

Get Access to over 20 more FREE Erotica Downloads at Shameless Book Deals

Shameless Book Deals is a website that shamelessly brings you the very best erotica at the best prices from the best authors to your inbox every day. Sign up to our newsletter to get access to the daily deals and the Shameless Free Story Archive!

LAST CHANCE AT THE MAN OF THE HOUSE BY ELIZA DEGAULLE

Amelia has long desired Paul, the man of her house. But when rumors of divorce begin to spring up, Paul might not be in her life for much longer. If she wants to make fantasy a reality, she has to act now. No time for preparations, no time for second thoughts, this is her last chance at the man of the house.

No one ever told me how lonely college could be.

Oh, you'll make lots of new friends they say, they'll be the best years of your life, and everything will be awesome.

Except, you know, when you kind of fail to connect with everyone except one or two people.

Sure, ultimately I was going just to get a degree for a better job and a better future, but that didn't change the fact that it wasn't the cure all I thought it was.

As I stepped out of the car and in front of my home again, I took a deep breath. Fresh air, sunshine. I missed this place.

Every day after high school was done, I'd rush home. I didn't want to miss him before he went off to work. School typically spit me out at 2:30, I could get home by 3, and he had to leave for work at 3:30.

Thirty minutes. Not long, but enough for a wonderful little chat that raised my spirits.

Who was 'him' you might ask?

Daddy.

Step-Daddy if you want to be specific about it, but I hadn't referred to him as that in years.

Or ever, really.

I never really knew my biological father, and Paul came into my life dating and then marrying my mother about ten years ago. All through those ten years, I've turned from a little girl into a young woman, one insecure about what the guys thought about her body and always second guessed if she was someone the boys even wanted to deal with.

Chubby. Frumpy. Doofy. I'd been called it all. My mother assured me they were just being mean, because self-hating bullies will so often lash out to berate others to make themselves feel better. Her words weren't as potent as his though.

I'd ask Daddy if a certain outfit looked cute, and he always gave me the affirmation I craved. Sometimes even without prompting, telling me that the boys should be lining up at the door, chasing me down, and playfully asking why I never brought a boyfriend home.

When I said I never had one, he said if I had a girlfriend, that was okay too, because they shouldn't be able to pass me up either.

Oh, that wasn't the reason I didn't have a boyfriend, mind you. That wasn't it at all. I was very much heterosexual and as I entered my home and looked out the back window, I saw my proof walking around that backyard, tending to the grass.

Shirtless too.

Oh boy. I was never so certain that I was heterosexual when I saw Daddy without his shirt on. He still hit the gym, but he definitely wasn't the type going and working out just to overinflate himself and pump up those glamour muscles that I heard them called.

No, him heaving up that lawnmower with one hand told me that his strength was very real.

Ever since I'd started to think about guys in that way, Daddy had been at the forefront of my fantasies. Wishing that he would come in here, sweep me off my feet, and carry me off to bed. That he would strip me naked, relish in how beautiful I was to him, and then he would take me.

Then he would make me scream as loud as he used to make Mommy scream.

Used to, anyway. It'd been a few years since, well, uh... I've been woken up by a woman's screaming.

That should have been terrifying, but I figured out what it was and ended up just jealous.

"Amelia. Ah, you're home."

My mother was behind me. She had a bit of a glow to her, and a smile to match. Had she just...?

"Hi, Mom," I said, turning around, dumping my backpack down and sitting on the window sill.

"Were you just watching Paul out there mowing the lawn?"

"Um... yeah."

She shook her head. "You know it's not proper that you look at him like that, right? He's your step-father."

"Oh, it wasn't that, Mom. I just missed Daddy. College has been stressful."

"I don't like you calling him that either."

"What, Daddy?"

"He's your step-father, Amelia."

I shrugged. "I didn't exactly know my birth father sooo..."

"Projecting your Daddy issues onto him?"

"Um... uh..." I blushed. "No, of course not."

She stepped beside me and watched him. "Just between me and you, because I don't want to catch you off guard... I... um..."

"What's up, Mom?"

"I don't think he's going to be your step-father for much longer, dear."

"Huh? Why?"

"He's really let himself go, don't you think?"

I raised an eyebrow in disbelief at her words. "Um, what?"

"Those saggy old eyes. His Dad bod. That gut of his. He doesn't even shave his chest for me anymore."

I stared at her. Then I looked out at Dad.

Was she going senile? She was a few years south of fifty, which to me seemed a little early to be losing her marbles.

All of those things? Well, they made him sexier to me. I guess he showed me what a real man is, and sometimes it isn't a hyper manufactured body that bathes in anti-aging cream every morning.

"Besides... I think I found someone else."

I looked at her with shock. "Huh? You're cheating on Daddy?"

"Amelia, he's not your Daddy. He's just...someone who I was with for awhile. People are living longer. People move on. It happens nowadays."

I couldn't believe what I was hearing.

"Why are you so surprised? Why do you care, even?"

I thought about launching into some passionate speech about how much Paul meant to me. How much Daddy meant to me. How he was there through my roughest years of growing up, and making sure my confidence didn't fall off a cliff after being pushed toward it in school every day.

How he got me through some lonely nights, and the thoughts of him made missing prom a little less painful.

All of that, though? I realized it was a little off. She was my mother. The woman who gave birth to me. Who raised me. Who took care of me. I should have instantly took her side, and yet?

"Oh, hey, Ami, you're home!" Daddy said, coming in, a wide smile on his face. "Come here and give me a hug."

I happily obeyed, keeping an eye levied at my mother.

She rolled her eyes and walked out of the room.

The smile on Daddy's face quickly faded when she left. "I don't know what's with her recently."

"Yeah, I don't know what's with her either." I shifted out of the hug. Being put in this situation so suddenly felt unfair. Did I lie to Daddy?

I hated having to play favorites.

"Well phooey to that. I'm just glad to see you home, sweetie. You getting along well at school?"

"Kinda, I guess."

He looked my way. "Is something bothering you?"

It was like he could read minds sometimes. "No, no, nothing about school is bothering me. I'm doing well. Good grades and all of that."

"You're going to flourish. Valedictorian?"

"I guess. Maybe?" I honestly had no idea. I thought I was doing well, but I had no idea how that compared to everyone else.

"Valedictorian it is, for you."

"Wow, now I have pressure on me. Thanks."

"It's a pressure of love. Or something." His hands on my shoulders, he was always such a loving man. He was the best father someone could ever ask for, and I was surprised my mother never gave him more kids, leaving me an only child.

With my mother saying he wasn't hot anymore though, all my mother's decisions were suddenly questionable.

"Ami, you go and settle back in. Your room is how you left it. I'm going to go and cook some burgers on the grill. Did you want some hot dogs too?"

"Um... yes, Daddy, I love hot dogs."

I always said that with a knowing grin.

Like, I legitimately liked the food, especially with how he made them.

Just. You know.

Hot dogs. A long tube of meat.

Like something else I wanted from him.

What I'm getting it as my step-father was hot and I wanted to fuck him.

Just laying that out in case you weren't following.

"Okay, Daddy. I'll go and get ready for dinner. Maybe I'll come down and help out."

"Nah, you're the reason for the celebration. Take it easy. It's your summer break."

I nodded his way, not really wanting to fight him to do more work.

Heading upstairs, I contemplated it all. I knew it was wrong to lust after him like this, and the thought of causing so much trouble with my mother for even suggesting such a thing was readily apparent to me.

Yet if they were to divorce and split...

Did I have that holding me back anymore?

∽

A HOT SHOWER, a new set of clothes, and I was relaxing on my bed with my phone, waiting for the call for hot dogs.

Catching up with my internet friends, checking in on the

news, whatever else. It was enough to get my mind off the whole Daddy and divorce thing that had been plaguing me.

Yet sometimes when you're trying to avoid something it'll remind you it's there with a vengeance.

"A divorce, Loretta? A divorce? Where the hell did this come from?" His booming voice echoed through the halls.

Oh boy. Mom had dropped that bomb.

"It's my right to want out of this marriage, Paul! We've been loveless for years!"

"Because you won't open up to me!"

"I don't want to open up to you!'

The shouting was loud, and really? This wasn't something I ever heard before. They fought. All couples do, it's inevitable. Up until now though, I assumed it was done in private, in the bedroom and wherever.

Not shouting down the hall.

What's next? Them throwing things?

As soon as that thought passed my mind, glass shattered.

Yep, they were throwing things.

"Christ, Loretta, what, are you trying to get me to call the police?"

"If that's what it takes to get a divorce!"

"What the hell is wrong with you, woman?"

"I'm sleeping with Tom, Paul! Tom makes me feel like a woman, something you haven't done in the longest time!"

"You won't let me make you feel like a woman!"

"Because I'm bored of you!"

"You shoot down all of my suggestions to change it up too! Like the thing with the um.. Christ, stop throwing things!"

Another thud followed up. I had no idea what was being used as the projectiles.

"Fine! I'm going to Tom's! I'll be back for you to wise up to tomorrow!"

"Loretta, hold up. Wait, what do I tell Amelia about..."

The sound of the front door slamming shook the house.

"About what's going on, and... Loretta?" The volume of his voice dropped.

I sighed. My mother took off without even telling me anything. She had her head in the clouds, and I guess the empty nest syndrome made her forget about me.

Shooting up, I headed down the stairs. If she wasn't going to talk to me about this, at least Daddy would.

Daddy was in the kitchen, picking up some broken glass off the floor.

"Let me help you with that," I said, rushing in.

"Woah, hold up. One, you have bare feet, and two, didn't I tell you you don't have to do housework right as your summer vacation begins?"

He flashed me a smile. He was so good at holding himself together even in the face of this chaos.

"You shouldn't have to clean her mess up though."

"Yeah, well, even if I wanted to let you, I direct you to my first point. You aren't dressed for this situation."

Stupid logic and easily cut feet. So I obeyed, and stayed back. "So... are you going to give it to her?" I said, meek and unsure of what I wanted to hear.

"Loretta? Oh. I guess I have to. There's no point in fighting something if she doesn't even want to try to make it work."

"What happened?"

He took a deep breath, and shuffled the broken plate into the trash can. "Should be clear now, Ami. I'm sorry, no hot dogs, I got side-tracked with your mother. I'll order you a pizza."

"Daddy, I asked you a question."

He remained silent. "Do you really want to know?"

"Yes."

"About your mother's love life?"

"Well, um... you don't have to describe that part."

He shrugged. "That's the main part I think is happening."

"Uh... it's cold in the bedroom I guess?"

"That's a metaphor to use, I suppose. Your mother hasn't been receptive to my advances in a few years now."

A few years? Does that mean it's been that long since he had a woman's proper touch?

"I thought it was menopause, or just a mid-life crisis. Maybe depression. I tried to ask her, I tried to be there for her, but she just kept pushing me away. That it led to this... I shouldn't be surprised."

Well, it had been a few years since I was rudely woken up by her screams of pleasure, so that lined up. For the longest time I thought I just got used to the sound and just slept through it.

"So, she hasn't been there for you in return?"

He shook his head. "I've suggested everything. New things in the bedroom. Seeing a counselor. When you went off to college, I said we should take a vacation. She shot it down."

This man. Mom was right about one thing, there was definitely a weariness to him. It may have been entirely her fault, however.

I went in to hug him. He seemed taken aback by this.

"What's wrong, Daddy?"

"I would think you would take your mother's side on this."

"Daddy, I can see things for what they are. She's being a bit of jerk and not even trying to make it work. I know you try, Daddy. You deserve better than her."

"Amelia, you know if I'm not married to your mother, than I'm not..."

"I don't care about that. You've always been there for me. You've always treated me right, given me the boost I need. You deserve better, Daddy."

Even as I said all this, I was very aware of my thoughts and fantasies that were rushing through.

"Why do you even still call me that?"

"Why wouldn't I? You take care of me. You're the man of the house. You're Daddy."

"Amelia, what's with you, anyway?"

During our conversation, I crept closer and closer to him. Getting more handsy. Invading that personal space.

No matter what I said or did, if what Mom wanted to do played out, he would be leaving my life. He said he'd keep in touch but we'd inevitably drift apart. We didn't have that bond of blood. Of romantic love.

Unless we could kindle such a fire between us.

"What's with what?"

"You're crawling all over me. You're like, one second away from hoping into my lap."

"Would that be such a bad thing?"

He stared at me in disbelief. "Are you trying to suggest something, sweetie?"

I nodded. "I'm being very suggestive right now."

"Um... if we were to do the thing that you may be suggesting we do, it would be very wrong, you know that right? I'm your father. Step-father."

"So no blood between us then, huh?"

"It's more than that. What would your mother think?"

"When do we care what she thinks?"

He shook his head. "She's your mother. I don't think she'd..."

"She doesn't want to be a part of this family, Daddy. The way I see it, we shouldn't have to worry about what she wants.

My time was running out. I never thought I'd make a move on him anyway. I always thought it'd be nothing more than a fantasy, but if he was eventually going to be leaving my life.

I had to try. Accepting me or rejecting me, it didn't matter.

"Amelia, doing the thing we're being suggestive would be wrong."

"What's wrong is Mom stringing you along for years when she lost interest. When she doesn't see how good you really are, Daddy. You're a man. You deserve a woman who really cares about you."

"Amelia, come on..."

He was protesting, but I wouldn't hear any more of it.

I kissed him.

To my surprise, he didn't immediately recoil.

Instead, he leaned into it. Kissing me back, his arms wrapping around me, pulling me close.

His lips on mine felt so damn good. I never thought kissing a man would feel like this, especially not him.

Finally, with clearly some effort on his part, he broke away from our embrace, gasping for air suddenly.

His eyes wide, he stared into mine. "You really can't want this, Amelia."

"I do," I said with a pant, "I really do. You're my first crush, Daddy. I've been so jealous of Mom at times, and I know it's wrong. But hearing how she's neglected and mistreated you? I don't care. It's either tell you how I feel now, Daddy, or I'm never going to see you again."

"There's no going back from this. We can't just go and pretend something like this didn't happen, no matter what we tell ourselves."

"I think we've already crossed a line, Daddy, so I say we embrace. We go all the way. Let me make you feel like a man again."

An audible swallow from him.

"There really is no going back from any of this. We can't forget this, it's out there. So..."

I kissed him again.

This time he was more receptive. My words had gotten through to him, and had spoken to his most base desires. The man that was inside Daddy, instead of the respectable father figure.

I straddled him and he leaned into it. His hands gripping my pajama bottoms, and into my ass. Digging into the softness of my flesh, and ran my hands down the firmness of his.

Wordlessly, he showed me that strength I had long admired by picking me up and carrying me away. Up the stairs. Toward the bedroom.

He planted me right on that mattress and looked down on me with amazement. "If I'm going to do this, I'm going to do this right. I'm not frivolously going to bend you over the table, Amelia. I'm going to fuck you good and proper."

All metaphor abandoned, I nodded. "Whatever Daddy wants, Daddy will get."

"Well, well, aren't you the people pleaser?"

"I'm the you pleaser, Daddy. This is something I've wanted for a very, very long time."

"And if your mother hadn't pulled the stuff she did..."

"I would have kept it quiet. Take it to my grave."

"But because she didn't..."

"It's her loss. I want you, and she was the only thing stopping me."

"Such a deviant little girl hiding under my roof all this time."

I gleefully nodded. If I had no morals or reservations I would have been making moves on him regardless of my mother's foolishness.

The words were said. He was sure I wanted this, as twisted as it was.

So we moved beyond kissing.

His big, beefy hands going down my body, to my shirt, hiking it up and over my head. My breasts fell free, as I had only dressed for lounging around the house, and that didn't typically call or wearing a bra.

Daddy's eyes rolled over them and he nodded. "You really have become quite the beautiful young woman, haven't you?"

All I could really do was blush.

He then did more than look, he felt. He moved his hands down my body, goosebumps forming anywhere and everywhere on me.

Daddy then touched my nipples, and the electricity ran through me all too instantly. Pleasure all too strong, things I've never felt. Sure, I've touched myself. I wasn't going to lie and say I've never explored my body and the joys that I could feel doing so.

The touch of a man, especially when it's one like him, blew away the rote enjoyment I got out of touching myself.

It wasn't just touch. There was a technique to it, a grace to go along with just the joy of his fingers on my most sensitive of parts. He tweaked them, massaged them, made me feel things that I never thought possible.

He marveled at my body, something that I thought no man would ever really do. He inspired me.

In strange ways, but I guess it was inspiration none the less.

Kicking down my pants, shuffling them over my butt, I wanted to show the rest of my body to Daddy, to see if would make him as proud as the top half of me.

"Aren't we the little firecracker? You just want it all and you want it now."

I nodded enthusiastically.

"Christ, you remind me of your mother in all the best ways. All of her best features... and somehow even better,

Amelia. You're such an enticing little vixen. It's something that I'm going to have to taste."

Taste? What did he mean by that?

His hands roamed down my body, across my thighs, into my valley, circling around my sex. He looked upon it and the smile on his face told me he was very much pleased with what he was seeing.

Years of shame, anxiety, and everything else were melting away. Just to see Daddy's approval, the only approval that truly seemed to matter to me.

He kissed me on the lips, and then departed them, going down my body bit by bit, continuing to kiss me all along the way. Across my neck, my chest. Going to my breasts, and suckling them ever so sweetly. The little bits of electricity shoot through me from there, but he isn't stopping. It's only a short detour in his main destination that was right between my legs.

Daddy's fingers were there first, sliding down my body, sliding across my nub. When he first touched my clit, I was surprised that I didn't simply cum from that alone.

He teased me there, watching me as it made me convulse. "My, my, you either are more inexperienced than I thought or you've really, really wanted this for quite some time."

"A little of column A, and a little of column B."

More inexperienced than he thought? How experienced did he think I was?

His fingers roamed my sex, sliding past my folds. I kept shuddering as he touched me, the feeling more intense than I ever expected.

"Amelia... are you a virgin?"

The color drained from my face.

I was sort of ashamed of that fact at this point in my life. I wasn't hyper religious or saving it for the right guy.

Or at least saving it for the right guy in the traditional sense.

Nothing about the man who I dreamed of saving it for was traditional.

I nodded though, answering Daddy's question.

To my surprise, he suddenly stopped, and sat at the edge of the bed. "We can't do this, Amelia."

"Why?" I said, shooting up. "Why not?"

"I can't take your virginity. It's not right."

Now he was getting second thoughts?

"Daddy... I thought maybe finding a guy would cure my sinful thoughts about you. But I just compared them all to you, and even the ones who showed interest in me I spurned... because I don't think I was ever going to give it to anyone but you, Daddy."

"Amelia, I can't..."

He tried to protest again, so I struck with another kiss.

In the short time of us just making out, he had taught me much. How to gracefully bring the tongue in, how to push a kiss deeper, and how a good kiss was done with more than just your mouth.

You leaned into your lover. You made them really relish in the fact you adored them.

The kiss broke. "Take me, Daddy. Please. Better you than some random jerk. I trust you, Daddy. You'll treat me right."

He paused again, but soon nodded. "Fuck, I'm already burning in hell, but dammit, Amelia, if I'm going to be your first, I need to make damn sure it's something you'll never forget."

"Oh trust me, Daddy, there's no way I'm forgetting this."

Another sudden kiss, sweeping me off my feet and pining me to the bed. This time he didn't linger with the romance as long, his kisses coming down my body swiftly, inching down me and coming to my sex once again.

His lips massaged against my clit so suddenly, and I almost exploded from the sudden spike of pleasure.

This was only the beginning, though.

His tongue slithered into my sex, pushing my folds apart, slurping up my juices. The intensity of what I was feeling was so powerful that I cried out all too suddenly.

There was a sly look on Daddy's face, liking what he was doing to me, pushing me higher as he worshiped me down there. Every lick, every stroke spiked me higher.

His tongue flicked in and out of me faster, and his hands? His hands were doing work. Massaging my clit, my breasts, anything and everything I was tossing and turning about. My own hands were just grabbing the blankets and sheets, trying to hold on, to endure what he was doing to my inexperienced body just a little bit longer.

Yet that inexperience was going to prevent me from truly savoring it. My poor self couldn't handle a man of Daddy's skill, who knew just how to make a woman melt into him.

My heart was racing, my blood was pumping, and my body was completely his. I couldn't help but melt into him, grab a bunch of Daddy's hair and scream, singing my praises for the wonders that were his mouth meeting my pussy.

Everything went momentarily white as I came, and my face flushing with the sweet ecstasy of orgasm. It lingered inside me for so long, and yet, it still wasn't long enough for me.

Soon, I was laying back on his bed, a sweating mess, panting for breath.

"I haven't heard a girl scream for me like that in years, Amelia. I forgot how sweet a sound that could be."

"How... how could she get tired of something like this, Daddy?"

Daddy shrugged. "I don't know, baby girl. People are

weird, and sometimes we don't understand them even if we think we know everything about them."

"I don't think I could ever get tired of you, Daddy."

"The same here, sweetie. The same here. But now.... now I have to have you."

"Have me?"

"You wanted me to take your virginity, right?"

I gasped, realizing we weren't even close to done. I nodded. "Please, Daddy. Show me everything."

"Oh, there's a lot more to sex than just what I'm about to do to you. I'll show you it all, but it'll take time. Tonight though, I'll ease you into the first sinful lessons of adult life."

I nodded enthusiastically, all too ready to learn the lessons he would teach me.

He stood tall before me, taking off his belt, and dropping his jeans down his legs. There was a hell of bulge poking out right between his legs.

Like, enough to intimidate me.

I think I'd established I wasn't a super pure virgin as one would think. I knew how sex worked.

But seeing Daddy's... uh... thing, well, it made me suddenly question the logistics of sex and how maybe everything I thought I knew was suddenly wrong.

I remained firm and hopeful though. Daddy wouldn't hurt me. I trusted him too much for him to start now just to get his rocks off.

Then, of course, he slid those boxer briefs down his legs too, and the cock proper sprung out.

Second thoughts passed through my mind, but again, I overcame them.

I laid back, shot Daddy my most sinful of glares, and then waved my finger at him.

"You sure you're a virgin? You're acting awfully..."

"Daddy, I was just doing what I saw in the movies."

"Oh. Well, sweetie, it's a whole lot more than what you see in the movies."

"Really?"

"Yes. How about I just show you?"

He jumped onto me, another kiss, his naked body pressing against mine. His cock throbbed against my thigh, and it inched ever closer to my purity.

To hell with it, I thought. I nodded toward Daddy, and urged him to take me already.

He looked into my eyes, seemingly trying to read me to make sure I was absolutely sure about this. Asking your father to take your virginity wasn't exactly something that you did lightly.

I'd never been more sure of anything though, and I hoped that shined through.

Feeling his cock roll against my body, tease my slit. My warmth rubbing against him.

I just nodded more. I needed this. He couldn't stop now.

He pressed himself in, and I felt myself part around him as he entered me. It was so immense feeling him inside me like that.

The sensation of him pressing in, the stretching of my sex around him, it strained me. This was a lot to take in, for lack of a better term. There was a slight bit of pain, but Daddy was there.

He caressed me. Cared for me. Made sure that there was far more pleasure than pain.

Deep within me, he waited for a time, let me adjust to the feeling of such a cock inside of me.

Like all things, I eventually got used to it. Unlike all things, I started to like it, and like it more and more.

I nodded his way again, just to let him know that I was fine, and more than ready for more of him.

So he took me. Properly.

Not too quickly at first, but definitely nonetheless. A steady pace rocking in and out of me, thrusting inside me. Going back and forth, going deeper and harder inside of me.

Every stroke was a wonderful and blissful rising tide. Every penetration took me higher.

I couldn't keep my mouth closed. Soon, I was singing for him. Moaning, groaning, whatever you wanted to call it, I was letting my approval be heard loud and clear.

Adjusting to the tryst, soon I was backing into him, grinding against him, fucking him back as he fucked me.

I heard him gasp in delight as I did my part. Hearing him like this, hearing his approval? It was a hell of a rush all in itself.

"Fuck, you're enthusiastic, Amelia."

"I've wanted you forever, Daddy. Please. Keep fucking me. Keep showing me. Take all of me, Daddy."

He nodded, and he threw himself into it even more.

Daddy's arms hooked under my knees as he took me deeper. His naked cock inside of me, fucking me powerfully and deeply.

It was then I realized that in my rush to seduce my father I had failed to take certain prrecautions.

Daddy was fucking me right now.

Nothing between us. Unprotected with full risks on the table. I wasn't on anything, and we didn't really discuss anything beforehand.

The shock of bliss that went through me right at that moment was a sharp reminder for me to not care about what was happening. I needed this, I wanted this. I'd give anything to have Daddy, even if it meant crossing another audacious line with him.

My fingers clawed at his back as I bucked into him, as he fucked me harder, as he fucked me deeper. The way he was taking me, it was like he wanted to knock me up. No reservations, just purely primal and visceral.

I loved it.

"Harder, Daddy, more," I said. Or at least I thought I said. Words and moans were blurring together at this point and it was hard to tell them apart.

Whatever he heard, he didn't stop. He was driven, his eyes firmly locked on mine as he fucked me. Determined yet kind.

I was getting near climax. I knew that much. It was stronger than anything I'd experience before, even from his tongue.

Harder. Faster. He was impaling me, and I would have it no other way.

I thought maybe I could hold on. Ride out this bliss just a bit longer, maybe.

Daddy was a cheater though. In the good way, mind you.

Seeing me on edge, he set forth to bring me home. His finger right on my nub, rubbing me, urging me to come.

There was no way I could turn such a request down, after all.

My entire body erupted in bliss. Every nerve inside of me was on fire all of a sudden and I could barely contain myself. I was slamming my hands on the mattress trying to stave it off, but it was no use.

I was his, totally and completely.

Screams, moans, I didn't know what I was doing as it truly felt as if I was in sensory overload at that point, and the other thing I could perceive was pure pleasure.

As I started to come down from my heights, I felt his grip on my hips tighten, his cock quiver inside me, and an eruption of warmth within.

He had cum inside me.

My mind was rushing with thoughts of what may have just happened, and yet...

I savored it. I relished it.

My arms around him, his arms around me, I was so entwined with him at that point, and it was absolutely perfect.

For a time, we sat there, just enjoying the moment. He was in no rush to leave me, and I didn't want him to leave.

He was a little slower to realize something than I did though.

Daddy slid himself out of me, but kept holding me. "I'm sorry."

"About what?" I said, barely above a whisper.

"I came inside you. I should have checked."

A smile came across my face. "That's fine, Daddy. You're worth every risk."

"You might get pregnant, Amelia."

"And? Would that be so bad?"

"You're nineteen."

"Young and fertile. Ready for anything."

"And you're in college."

I smirked his way. "With you, Daddy, everything will be fine, no matter what happens."

He held me tighter. "You're just a seductive little vixen aren't you."

"Anything for you, Daddy." The smile on my face hadn't faded for quite some time.

"Really, I'm surprised you're okay with it. Your mother never wanted..."

"Amelia? Paul?" A voice that wasn't ours called out.

Together, we rolled to face the door of the room. We thought we were alone, and there was no reason to take a precaution like closing the door.

Looking right at both of us, absolutely horrified, was my mother.

"What... what are you doing?"

"Hi Mom," I said, not wanting to leave his arms.

"Paul, what's the meaning of this?"

Daddy was red in the face. "Loretta... a man has needs. You didn't want to fulfill them, so Amelia offered to instead."

Her eyes wide, her shock hadn't subsided.

She couldn't take anymore of this, turning and fleeing.

Daddy let out an annoyed breath. "She'll be fine."

"You're the only one that matters to me now," I said.

"And the same for me, sweetie."

He kept on holding me, as if my mother hadn't walked in on us.

It turned out hearing my mother's desire for divorce was the best thing to ever happen to me.

Everything I ever wanted, everything I ever desired had finally come true, and Daddy was mine now.

As I felt his seed leak out of me, the smile on my face grew stronger.

No matter what happened, I would face it head on, and he would be there with me.

Caring for me. Protecting me.

And truly making me feel like a woman.

THE END

Get Access to over 20 more FREE Erotica Downloads at Shameless Book Deals

Shameless Book Deals is a website that shamelessly brings you the very best erotica at the best prices from the best authors to your inbox every day. Sign up to our newsletter to get access to the daily deals and the Shameless Free Story Archive!

PLANT IT IN MY GARDEN, DADDY BY KIMMY WELSH

My Step-Daddy Charlie and I are working hard in the heat, landscaping the garden so my Mom can enjoy the sunshine in seclusion. She brings us a drink and dotes on him before leaving the two of us alone. When Charlie removes his t-shirt I can't help but get excited by the site before me, and now I want him to treat me just like her.

It's so wrong to be taking him from her like that, but I'm determined to get what I want most of all—and what I want right now is for him to plant himself deep and let it all out inside me. I'm gonna get what I want no matter how naughty it is.

"We'll be done before the weekend's out, Maddie" Charlie said, stabbing his shovel into the dirt and tossing another clod on the growing pile.

"You think?" I asked, surprised. Looking around it seemed as though we'd only just started, and the heat really didn't help things.

He scanned the garden and hummed. "I kind of promised your mother."

"Good luck," I laughed.

Charlie had been living with us for almost five years now after Dad left. If I'm honest, I considered him the perfect replacement, but nevertheless I still had a problem calling him 'Daddy,' not least because I kind of thought he was sexy.

"I need it," Charlie said, blowing a jet of air up his face so that the front of his brown hair shot up.

"Who's thirsty?" came Mom's voice as she sauntered up the secluded garden's path with a jug of lemonade.

Charlie wiped his brow and speared his shovel into the dirt, smiling at Mom as she approached him.

They kissed like it was the first time they'd seen each other in weeks and I felt a pang of jealousy at their bond. I wished I could get my hands on Charlie the exact same way. He treated Mom so special, and I wanted to experience that too.

"Madison," Mom said, smiling as she gave me a drink.

"Thanks," I said quietly, taking the drink from her and feeling the pang of jealousy slowly dissipate.

"I'm popping out for a couple of hours," she said. "But when I get back I expect you two to have finished."

She wagged a finger and then a smirk broke out on her face.

"We'll be lucky to get a quarter of it done today," I said, looking around.

"We'll try our damndest," Charlie said. "Anything for you, my love."

Charlie kissed her again and I rolled my eyes. "Jeez, guys."

He looked over at me and the twinkle stayed in his gaze. I felt a twist in my stomach as I caught a brief glimpse of the look that was reserved only for Mom. My insides started to melt.

"You two be good," Mom said, but I was now beginning to think I had no such plans.

She walked away, looking back over her shoulder at Charlie who followed her the whole way down the garden until she slipped in through the back door again.

He gave a contented sigh and then picked up his shovel, going straight back to work with a lingering smile on his face.

I watched him a while, seeing those sweaty arms of his flex in the hot sun. If Charlie looked hot before, then the addition of dirt, sweat and sunshine really sent him off the charts.

I looked down at myself by way of comparison. I had on a pair of short shorts and old sneakers, with a white, now-dirty tank-top on my upper half. Despite this I still felt the heat. Feeling the attraction to Charlie only wound up making me less comfortable.

"It is *hot*," he announced after several more minutes of heavy digging.

Without a word he pulled his t-shirt up over his head and I damn near swallowed my tongue when I watched his washboard abs creep out from underneath his top.

I stopped working to stare at him, losing myself in his body like it was a maze for the eyes. I remember thinking that I should be looking at his face at some point, but I couldn't stop trailing my gaze over him.

Despite being over forty he had a body that looked like it belonged to someone half his age. His chest was smattered with just enough hair to make me wanna push my fingers through it. I was a virgin and I think that's why I lusted for him even more. At nineteen I felt as though I needed the calm, commanding confidence of an older man to really guide me through the experience.

"Tired?" he asked, and it caused me to jolt from the

daydream. I started to blush as I realized how long I'd been staring.

"Just having a breather," I said, swallowing hard and trying my damndest now to not look at that magnificent physique of his.

The second Charlie resumed his work I was back on him, watching the sweat drip over the contours of his skin and imagining that I had the same access to his body as Mom did. *How could I get closer to him?*

As I toiled away slowly a thought struck me. At first it seemed so child-like in its simplicity, but it was a perfectly innocent offer that would grant me an intimate proximity. I tossed down my shovel and headed back for the house.

"Lunch break already?" Charlie said.

"I'm just going to get something," I called back.

His brow furrowed but he continued his work in my absence. He'd have done the whole gig by himself if it meant pleasing Mom.

Inside the house I searched frantically for the sunscreen, finding it eventually beneath the sink in the bathroom and holding it aloft like it was some kind of sacred relic.

I sauntered back out into the garden with a broad smile. "Let me put some of this on you," I said, shaking the bottle. "Don't want you getting burnt."

Charlie narrowed his eyes. "Good point," he said, and I felt the relief and excitement wash over me in equal measure.

"Turn around," I said.

"I got it," Charlie said, reaching his hand out for the bottle.

"I insist," I countered.

He tensed his jaw and turned away from me. "Right you are."

My smile widened as I scanned that big, broad back of his and squirted a dollop of cream into my palms. I rubbed them together eagerly and closed my eyes as my hands touched his skin. I started to rub it in slowly in tiny circular motions that moved across his shoulders and down his back.

"Mmm," he soothed, and it sounded though he hadn't intended to make the noise.

"Let's get it all rubbed in," I said absent-mindedly, feeling my body start to respond to him.

As I pushed the cream around his back and rubbed it into his muscles I felt my breath shorten and my stomach twist in excitement. My pulse rose and the lust pumped through me.

"There we go," I said slowly, adding more sunscreen to my palm and sliding it up and down the side of his body. "Turn around and I'll do your front."

"I got it," Charlie said.

"My hands are already greasy," I said. "I don't mind."

Charlie turned slowly. "If you're sure," he said.

I felt the nerves almost overpower me as he faced me. Now I was desperately trying to hide my lust, casing my eyes downwards so that he couldn't see the dilation in my pupils.

I didn't notice it at first. Instead I looked back to his face, realizing when I glanced to him that he too seemed nervous. Without thinking I squirted the cream into my hands again and that's when I saw the source of his sudden discomfort.

There, in his shorts, lay a big, thick column of flesh. It moved from the middle of his pants, out to the side, somewhere below his pocket. He was clearly aroused—of that there was no doubt. So aroused, in fact, that it felt stranger *not* to address it.

I rubbed my palms on his chest and continued to stare at his crotch. I licked my lips and closed my eyes as I ran my hands over his pecs and down his body. My fingers teased a little way inside the waist of his shorts and I heard him suck a sharp breath through his teeth before I moved my hands back to a more permissible location.

"Maddie, I—"

"I need to make sure it's all rubbed in," I said, refusing to stop.

I took a step neared to him as I massaged his torso, putting my head and face dangerously close to his own.

He cast his head downwards and I could hear his breath close to my ear. Again I teased at the waist of his pants, then I steeled my nerves and made a grab for that beautiful package of his.

I touched at the stiff flesh and Charlie recoiled, taking a step back. "Maddie, I'm not sure we should be doing this."

"Neither am I," I confessed. "It just feels like I have this urge for you that I can't control."

"I know," Charlie said, and I was taken aback. "I know because I've felt it too."

The sudden announcement confused me.

"It's so hard having you so close to me with so few clothes on," he continued. "Any man would struggle."

I looked down myself, surprised. I hadn't imagined my dirty little tank-top and old shorts would be in any way sexy, but I guess I was wrong.

"You don't have to struggle," I said, moving closer to him.

"Your mother," he said.

"I know. I know but I don't care."

His eyes widened.

"I've never wanted anything more in my life," I said. "I deserve it."

"You deserve ... *me?*"

"I do," I said defiantly. "And you deserve me. You deserve *this.*" I looked down myself as I said the words, keen for Charlie to drink me in too.

"Maddie ..." he began, and I decided to play my ace-in-the-hole.

"I want you, Daddy."

When the word struck his ear his back straightened.

"I want you, *Daddy*," I repeated.

Charlie said nothing, standing there flummoxed. It was though the word was a key to his libido.

I swallowed nervously in the silence, moving my hand to the bottom of my tank-top and toying it in my fingertips. I started to lift the bottom slowly, revealing my stomach and more.

Charlie said nothing. I'd half-expected him to stop me in my tracks, but instead he watched as I pulled the top up over my head and revealed my pert tits to him.

I tossed the garment to the floor. The high fences surrounding the garden meant that Charlie and I were pretty secluded. We could do *anything*.

I took several breaths and Charlie watched my tits as they rose and fell on my chest. I could see the lust for them in his eyes and wondered if it was necessary to grant him permission.

Before I could say anything he stepped towards me and touched his hand to my bare breast, feeling its ripeness and closing his eyes as though he was fighting against something greater than himself.

I let out a soothing moan of acceptance and he brought another hand to my tits that moved around to my back and then my ass.

He stepped into me and squeezed at my tight butt, putting his forehead against mine. "I want you," he said.

I opened my mouth and put it on his lips. At first nothing happened but gradually he started to move and I broached my tongue over the divide, finding his in his mouth and twisting around it.

He sucked a breath through his nose and switched gears, injecting an added passion to the kiss. His waist pressed against me and I could feel that thick cock of his on my thigh. I felt safe in his arms, but I wanted much more than a kiss.

"Treat me like Mom," I said, taking my lips off his. "I want to do all the things to you that she does."

I started to kiss his face and then his neck, moving down to his glossed, hairy pecs and fondling at them as I continued my descent. Charlie's hands hung submissively at his sides and he watched me go down on him.

My hand pulled at the waist of his shorts and popped open the button effortlessly. The zipper slid down without complaint and his shorts fell to his ankles.

I rubbed at the thick cylinder of flesh that stretched beneath his boxer-shorts, teasing the both of us as and getting a good feel of his size.

When I was ready I curled my nails down inside the waist of his boxer-shorts and started to drag them down too. I watched the hair thicken as his underwear lowered, then the thick hilt of his cock became visible.

I swooned and my heart fluttered as more and more of his engorged inches were revealed. Eventually his hard cock rolled out of the top of his Calvins and hung there, suspended with arousal and waiting to be claimed.

I sat back on my heels and covered my mouth. His cock was huge. I'd never seen one quite so close before and the thing looked almost menacing in its size. A thick vein ran up the side of it. I don't mind admitting that it was intimidating.

"He doesn't bite," Charlie said, taking his cock in his hand and giving it a playful bounce.

I moved back to him, watching close at the swollen, soft-pink crown. The hue of his cock was inviting me onto it. I just had to taste it.

I grabbed it from him and Charlie looked down his body expectantly, moving my hair aside and taking a look deep into my eyes.

Kneeling at his feet like that and staring up at him felt like heaven. I was in a place I'd longed dreamt about, only this time it was for real. Everything that was about to happen was real. I wasn't in dreamland any longer.

My mouth opened tentatively and I moved towards Charlie's cock, clearly much slower than he'd liked. When I was an inch or so away he pushed his hips forwards and suddenly I found his girth forcing my mouth open.

Before I knew it I could feel the pulse of his cock against my tongue. The blood beat into him over and over. I rolled my tongue along the underside of his shaft and tried not to smile when I heard the resultant groan escape him.

"That's good," he said, holding my head and leaning his face back to the sky.

I started to move my lips over him, jerking him in my mouth like I'd heard so many of my friends talk about. My hand would move over the exposed hilt of his cock every so often, but mostly I teased and circled the head of his dick with my tongue, clasping my lips tight around his shaft whenever it felt necessary.

Charlie clearly didn't mind. The more he moaned and groaned the more my confidence grew. I knew in no uncertain terms that he loved what I was doing to him.

I continued to pump his flesh inside me, closing my eyes and really getting into it. I concentrated on how hard and thick his cock felt, and how good it would feel to have it inside me. I took him from my mouth now and beat him in my fist, watching his freshly wet cock move under my spell.

"Oh, I want it," I moaned, staring at it as it shook in my hand.

"You're gonna get it," Charlie promised. "You're gonna get every last drop."

I realized then that he meant his cum, and it was the first time I'd considered the idea of his climax. As I thrust him back into my mouth I imagined the cum pouring from the tip of his cock, and then I imagined where it might be falling on me.

At first I imagined him coating my face as I sat on my knees, but then I started to imagine him pumping it all over my tits and finally I thought about him doing it inside me. How naughty a notion that was.

The last option started to make my chest red with desire. I knew as soon as the thought blossomed inside me that that was where I wanted it. I knew that he must have done the same to Mom in the past, and I wanted the exact same treatment. I wanted to feel him explode in me and know that it was all my doing.

"I want you to fuck me, Daddy," I said, using that magic-word freely now.

"You think you can handle it," Charlie said, squeezing the base of his dick as he pulled it from my mouth.

I looked again at the swollen cock, noticing how pronounced the veins in it were now that held it tight.

"I'm gonna try," I said, standing up.

Charlie kissed me and I grabbed his dick, stroking it and kissing his mouth as he moaned. He brought his hands back to my ass and pulled me against him so I couldn't move, then he kissed me deep and used two hands to press my body against his.

His cock teased at my waiting pussy. I could feel the moisture inside it and I knew that I was wet and ready. I'd need all the lubrication I could muster to get him inside of me, but at the minute that didn't seem like much of a demand. I was practically dripping for him.

Charlie stepped all the way out of his shorts until he was wearing only his desert-boots. It looked surreal to see him stood in the garden like that, as well as hot as hell. I never imagined that this would be where we did it.

"Take them off for me," he said and he leaned back against the wooden fence and watched.

I turned away from him and looked back over my shoulder as I peeled my shorts down. The whale-tail of my panties was slowly revealed and I rolled the pants down over my ass until he could see the whole thing.

Charlie jerked his cock as he watched, no doubt imagining all the things he wanted to do to me.

"Hurry," he said. "I want you back over here on my cock."

I quickened my movements, going to my panties and pulling them down so he could see the full majesty of my ass. It was another part of me that I was proud of, having put the hours in at the squat rack. Now it was paying off in dividends.

My panties rolled in my shorts and I stepped out of them both, turning to him in my sneakers. We both looked like a pair of naturalist, nude out there in the summer's sun.

I walked towards that big, hard cock of his, eager to see what he was going to do with it.

"You're in charge, Daddy," I said, making it known that I wanted him to dominate me.

"Come here," he said, and he turned me against the fence, pushing me onto it.

My hands met the top of it and I gripped it as my back arched, pointing my ass out towards him. Charlie kissed my shoulder and then my back, and quickly I realized where his mouth was headed.

He bit at my ass and soon he was tonguing under my asshole at the creamy pot of my pussy.

"So wet already," he said. "Is that all for me?"

"All for you, Daddy," I groaned, closing my eyes as he planted his lips on my pussy again.

His nose poked at my ass and gave me a thrill of added excitement as his tongue busied itself around my sensitive petals. He ate from me hungrily, making loud smacking noises and moans that let me know how much he enjoyed my body.

My anticipation was palpable when his mouth finally broke off my pussy and he stood up behind me. I knew now that there was only one more thing for him to do.

"Fuck me, Daddy," I begged, looking back to him with a sultry, slutty gaze.

"You want it?" he asked, wielding it in his hand like a weapon.

"Stick it in my pussy."

He smiled wryly and put a hand on my shoulder, using the other one to guide the tip of his cock to my waiting groove.

I used my hands to split my ass apart, making it easier for him to seek out the wet, tight spot of my sex.

"Do it," I said with breathy anticipation.

The moment was upon me. Charlie was about to claim my virginity and he had no idea. Just then I felt the smooth head of his cock begin to press into me and my mouth dropped open in a silent moan.

His dick stretched me wide and I threatened to cry out in pain, feeling the skin pull impossibly tight as he warmed me up.

"Fuck!" he exclaimed, clearly pleased by the grip of my muscle on his.

He surged onwards, driving up inside me against the tightness of my pussy. Finally, I let out a gasping breath, following it were several quick bursts of oxygen that felt necessary to quell the brief pangs of pain.

"That's it," he soothed, continuing to feed his inches into me until his hips touched against my ass.

I let go of my cheeks and they gripped against him too, keeping him in place.

"Now fuck me," I said defiantly.

He withdrew and I yelped, still not quite accustomed to his swollen girth.

"Yes, baby," Charlie said, seemingly spurred on by my cries.

He took my hair in his fist and yanked at it as he drove into me, starting to dominate me now, just like I wanted.

"Yes! Yes! Yes!" I growled, determined to battle through it.

Gradually the initial pain subsided and my pussy relaxed around him. With nothing now to tarnish the experience I concentrated on how well he filled me. It was so satisfying to be around him, as though I'd had this vacant spot my entire life and now that it was filled I felt complete.

He moved his chest against my back and stretched an arm under my own to grip at my shaking tits. "Where do you want it, babe?"

"Inside me," I hushed, bouncing against the fence as he thrust against me.

"That's *dangerous*," he said, biting at my ear.

"I know," I confessed. "But I need it."

There was a brief pang of guilt that thankfully vanished before it took root. Here I was, fucking my Mom's husband and my Step-Daddy, and more than that I was going to take his cum from him—take his cum from *her*—and let him plant it deep in my pussy. I was a *bad* girl.

"Come here," Charlie said, guiding me away from the fence. He walked close behind me, still keeping his cock inside me and leading me forward by the hair.

I moved with quick, short steps as he wrangled me into position. He found the wooden table-bench and pushed me over it. My tits pressed against the hot wood and he struck me from a new angle, sending his cock so deep that I didn't know it was possible to go that far inside me.

I yawned my mouth open in a silent moan as he explored me, jutting out my jaw and letting out a long growl.

"Yes!" I grunted, then his hips began to clap against my ass as he started to fuck me all over again.

I bounced forwards off him and he held my hips tight, squeezing at my ass as he watched his thickness disappear inside the impossibly small aperture.

His thumb pressed against my asshole and he split my cheeks to watch the majesty of the act. I looked back at him with a dirty smile, relishing the sensation of his digit teasing at my forbidden knot.

"Fill me up," I goaded, my face pressed against the table.

Charlie pulled my hair back and lifted my face off the table, slamming into me and then slapping my ass with his other hand.

The muscle of my pussy tightened on him and then I felt the rushing sensation of climax, creeping up on me like a thief.

"Right there," I groaned, keen to keep the sensation.

He wound my hair around his fist and slapped my ass again. This time my pussy contracted and sent a convulsion through me that seemed to awaken something.

Suddenly I was breathing hard and deep, feeling the orgasm flourish and take root.

"Oh, Daddy!" I cried, my vision swirling with intense colors as the sensations became overwhelming.

I breathed in so hard and deep that my head turned light and my scalp prickled like static. I'd barely even noticed how erratic Charlie was becoming.

"I'm coming, Daddy," I cried, keen for him to know what he'd done to me.

No words came back. Instead his hips crashed against my ass and he fed his length into me over and over, hitting a speed that was surely unsustainable as my pussy massaged him.

My eyes rolled back and I bounced beneath him like a submissive rag-doll.

"Give it to me," I grunted. "Give me your cum!"

Just then he let out a quick breath of relief, as though he'd been holding back. His thrusts slowed and his cock seemed to grow bigger.

"Here it comes," he said, and I barely had time to brace myself.

Suddenly I felt the throb of his dick, combined with a strained, guttural moan.

"Cum in my pussy," I urged.

My insides turned hot with his love as it blasted in to me. Quickly I felt the rush of his cream as it filled me, coating my insides and going deep into my core.

Each blast of cum came with an added groan of satisfaction as he steadily fucked me, sensually squeezing his cock through my tight, cum-glossed pussy.

"Every drop," I begged, keen not to waste any of my hard-fought reward.

Daddy did as I asked, and I felt the throbs wane and the rushes of cum lessen. He rounded off the act with a final, long groan, holding the hilt of his cock and dragging it out of me slowly.

I sucked in a breath as the bulbous crown popped out of me, followed soon-after by a dripping string of his love. I giggled and rubbed it back against my pussy, keen not to waste any of it.

"My God," he said, standing back and admiring the mess he'd made.

I looked back from the table and bit a finger, giggling with embarrassment. I couldn't believe we'd done it. I couldn't believe what was inside me.

Afterwards came the post-sex guilt that I'd thought was a myth. Suddenly I had a flash of my mother and then I panicked when I considered that his seed might take root inside me. *What would we do then?*

To combat the guilt the thrill of the act came back tenfold. I dragged myself off the table and span on my knees towards him, hungry to cleanse him of every last drop of his precious cum.

"Jeez!" he exclaimed, but he didn't stop me when I mouthed over the tip of his cock again.

I sucked on it and looked up into his eyes, lovingly racing my tongue around his shaft as he held my face tenderly.

"That's it," he said slowly.

I made a ceremony of pulling him from my mouth, squeezing my lips against him to drag every last bead of his seed from him. Afterwards I smacked my lips and fingered an errant drop into the corner of my mouth.

"Thank you, Daddy," I said, batting my lashes at him.

"You're a naughty girl," he said, absolving himself of the guilt.

"I am," I confessed.

"Naughty girls get punished."

"You can punish me any time, *Daddy*," I said, injecting one last bit of sass into proceedings.

I rose to my feet demurely, belying the acts we'd just committed. Charlie watched as I stepped back up into my shorts and pulled them up my legs as though nothing had happened.

"Back to work, huh?" he said, claiming his shorts and scrambling them over his boots.

"Work and play," I said.

We watched each other dress and the reality of what we'd done lingered in the background. If Mom were to find out, we'd both be finished. Again the guilt of it all threatened to eat me, but instead I concentrated on how good it had felt. Whenever the green-eyed-monster reared its head I'd focus on the pleasure we'd experienced together. I considered it a gift. I just hoped the experience would be the only gift I received, and not, instead, a new-born baby to worry about. I prayed we'd get away with it. I prayed she'd never find out.

THE END
Get Access to over 20 more FREE Erotica Downloads at Shameless Book Deals

Shameless Book Deals is a website that shamelessly brings you the very best erotica at the best prices from the best authors to your inbox every day. Sign up to our newsletter to get access to the daily deals and the Shameless Free Story Archive!

FOR MY OWN GOOD BY ZOE MORRISON

Mia's daddy is doing everything in his power to make sure her marriage lasts.

"I LOVE YOU!" My husband slurred, as he proceeded to drunkenly slide down the leather sofa, curl up like a contented fat cat and fall asleep on the floor in the lobby of the hotel.

My wedding day had been everything that I had ever wished for; it was my 19th birthday, the weather was warm and dry, my dress made me feel like a princess, and the flowers in the church looked absolutely wonderful. All that was left was for me to lose my virginity to my new loving mate and I was rarin' to go, but now as I gazed down at my husband of 9 hours softly snoring through his hard-earned and (I thought) well-deserved fuck away, my spirits were deflating. I had been looking forward to this day for over a year now and had purposely waited for this very day to give my all (in a manner of speaking.)

My dad, Dave, step-dad really but I loved him like my own, came and put his arm around my shoulder, and said, "I'll take him to bed, for you. Rick, grab an arm!" he shouted to his best friend of over twenty years. They then dragged my husband through the hotel lounge, leaving me to say goodnight, and apologize, to the last few of our guests with a red face and disappointment instead of elation as a girl's wedding day should be.

Marco had been drinking since breakfast, and the champagne, wine and beer had finally taken its toll. When he was this drunk, Marco, would sleep like a baby, until 10 or 11 o'clock the next morning. As that depressing thought set in and I was trying to accept that my wedding night was not going to be the way I had imagined it, I heard my dad bring me out of my trance.

"Where do you want him?" Dave asked, as we entered the bridal suite. "On the bed, I suppose," I replied.

After they had, unceremoniously, dropped him onto the bed, Rick said "that motherfucker is heavy, I'm going back to the bar." He then exited without a look back. Dad then asked me, "Should I undress him?" Again I replied, "I suppose so."

Dave was divorced from my mom but he had always been there for me when my mother married him, and as they maintained a good relationship after the divorce, he was present at my wedding to give me away. Dave was always good looking in a rugged sort of way that a lumberjack was in contrast to Marco who was looked more like his mother, small, thin and very pretty.

I was sitting on the sofa, feeling very sorry for myself, when dad handed me a glass of champagne, from our bottle, next to the bed. He very sadly smiled and said, "I'm sorry, my dear, but, you're going to be disappointed, on your wedding night." As he pulled down Marco's pants he added, "Looking at the size of his cock, you're going to be disappointed every night! Jesus Christ! My balls are bigger than that!" Dave laughed.

"I hope that he's good with his tongue, 'cos a little thing like that won't satisfy a beautiful girl like you." Dave said, looking me straight in the eye, smiling. "What do you mean?" I stammered. "You know…" and he wiggled his tongue. "Oh, my God no!" I gasped, and held my hand up to my face to hide my embarrassment. By now he was sitting next to me. "You mean he's never tasted your nectar, and made you scream like a banshee?" he quizzed me. I shook my head. "Never?" Again I shook my head.

"I don't believe it; If he doesn't go down, on a gorgeous young girl like this, and that's all he has," pointing to Marco's sad little cock, "You'll be fucking anything that moves, before Christmas, girls like you have got to be kept satisfied." "Next, you'll be telling me that he's the only man that you've ever been fucked by." I couldn't believe what I was hearing, and took another gulp of champagne, and shook my head no. "You mean to tell me that you've never done it? Not even with him?" I shook my head again and felt my face turning red. "I wanted to wait and Marco respected that." "You don't think that all men are that size, do you?" I shrugged my shoulders. Dave laughed.

It was true, Marco was my first real boyfriend, I had met him four years previously, when I was 15 and he was 19. Because he was old enough to be arrested for being with a girl my age he didn't push when I held back and he was understanding when messing around went too far and I asked him to stop. He was always a gentleman and I appreciated that as he liked the fact that I was a lady. When I graduated high school he was graduating college and he proposed to me. I agreed to marry him but I told him I wanted to get one year of college behind me first. He agreed and here we were.

Dave had a reputation with women long before he met my mom. Usually with young barmaids, which caused the breakdown of many a relationship. When he met my mom he finally got what he said he always wanted, a family. I was only a baby at the time but for over 15 years we were a family. But a leopard can't change its spots so it wasn't long before Dave was back to his old tricks again and after one affair too many, my mom had enough and called it quits.

Something about Daddy Dave though was very likable and you couldn't help but love him. After a fairly brief time apart, mom still had a soft spot for him and would often let him stay at our house for long weekend. He was the only daddy I had ever known so in spite of everything, for all intents and purposes, we were still a family.

Turning to face me, he started to unzip his fly, and pulled out his massive penis, it was about 7 inches long, soft, and as thick as my wrist. My eyes nearly popped out, and my jaw fell open. "You can touch it, if you like," he said as he winked at me.

Tentatively I stroked it with one finger, then it jerked, and I pulled my hand away. As I was staring at this magnificent object, it grew larger and harder, before my very eyes, until it was about 9 inches long. "Get a proper hold," he whispered as he placed my hand back onto his cock. Again, I stroked it, and the feeling was wonderful, as I had my whole hand wrapped around the shaft, and began to rub up and down, "grip it tighter and rub it faster," he commanded, I did as I was told.

"What do you think?" Dave asked.

I couldn't stop myself, "It's so big, it's wonderful." I continued wanking him.

"If you think this is something, you should see it in action!"

Dave stood up and removed his trousers, he began

walking towards me, his cock jutting out like a large cigar, dark in color, and at this point, about 10 inches long, instinctively, I put both my hands out to hold it and immediately began wanking with both hands.

My head was spinning, it was my wedding night, my new husband was naked and snoring on our bed, but here I was jerking my stepdad off in the same room. My head said stop, this wasn't right, but my body wasn't listening.

Dave moved closer, "Put you tongue out," I did, and he rubbed the tip of his cock along it, then around my ruby red lips. "Open wide!" He said, laughing. I complied and gently, he slipped his cock into my mouth. I was surprised that there was no taste or smell, but the action of having a cock in my mouth, had my fanny tingling and my nipples hard as buttons.

Daddy Dave put his hands along the side of my head, and stroked my hair, and wedding veil, as he moved his hips, gently pushing himself in and out of my mouth, "Suck it like a lollipop" he whispered, and I did.

Dave moved my hand off his own cock, and began pulling the zipper down, on my wedding dress, and unclipped my bra. While I continued sucking him, Dave pulled my dress down to expose my breasts. With both hands he began stroking my small breasts and nipples, which felt like bullets.

"That's enough," Dave said as he withdrew his cock from my mouth, "any more of that and I'll shoot!"

"Stand up," Dave told me, as I did so, my wedding dress fell to the floor, leaving me in my shoes, seamed stockings and matching silk panties and suspender belt, which had small pink bows on.

"Wow! You look fucking lovely," Dave said, "I'm trying to remember when the last time that I saw tits that pointed up like that?" I picked up my glass and smiled as I took a sip, reveling in my sexiness, while Dave stared at my body, and made comments in the crudest of terms, as he finished getting undressed.

~

As he was in his fifties, his body was a little quite soft, but he looked fantastic, as his long cock pointed at me from neatly trimmed pubic hair.

Moving my dress to one side and holding it up as I walked, Daddy gently pushed me back onto the sofa in the room, were I sat down and he sat beside me. He tenderly kissed me, then guided my head down to his thick and bulbous knob. I gripped onto the shaft as I opened my mouth to take the first couple of inches in, I felt like a whore as I began bobbing my head, forcing as much lovely cock into my mouth as I could take, sucking like my life depended on it. I felt Dave softly stroking my tits, then, my nylon clad legs. He pulled my left leg onto the couch on the other side of me which left my legs wide open, giving him unhindered access between my legs.

His fingers gently stroked my crack, making me shiver, with excitement. Still sucking on Dave's thick cock, I moved my hips and bottom, so he could slide my panties off me without having to give up that sweet prick. When they were off, I immediately placed my legs in the same position so that everything I had was open for the taking. I had never felt this horny before, and my ass was throbbing, to prove it. After a few more minutes of going down on Dave's cock, he stopped me and stood up. He pushed me down so that I was on my back then got back on top of me so that I was enjoying my first 69 ever. He said by stopping for a few minutes it gave him time to calm down because he wanted this to last awhile. Once he was in front of my goodie bag on top of me, he lightly blew on my nether regions sending a shiver up one way and down another throughout my body. Spreading my legs as wide as they would go, he just looked for a moment. "Oh baby, your cunt's winking at me!" he said as he slid one, then two fingers into my dripping love box. The dirty talk was turning me on, as much, if not more, than the actions.

His fingers were now going in deeper than my own had ever done. It felt so good I had to take the cock out of my mouth, as I was struggling to breathe. As Dave continued jamming his fingers into me, he moved his head down and start sucking on my 'special button' with the pressure of a vacuum while his other hand found my butthole and just barely rimmed the entrance; that was all that was needed though. With only two or three strokes, I was screaming like the 'banshee' that daddy had promised. So much so that he once again had to stuff my mouth full of cock to keep my husband from waking up.

I couldn't believe it! All that and technically I was still a virgin. As daddy got up off me and sat back on the couch, I flopped across his lap to reach for the champagne bottle for another nip. Dave took a swig after me then turned to me a said, "Now it's my turn," with that he got up and knelt at the end of the sofa, opening my legs, and aiming his monster at my entrance, "No, no daddy, no, I shouldn't, *we* shouldn't…" I whimpered, but my whole body was screaming, *"FUCKME! FUCKME! FUCKME!"*

"It's too late too worry about your reputation now!" Dave chuckled as he played with my tits, and I played with his heavy balls. He slowly nudged his cock against my hole, then slid it inside, in one long shove. It made me moan with first pain but it was quickly replaced with groans of pleasure, as it filled my body, like nothing had never been filled before. With my legs so wide apart, Dave was sliding in and out with the greatest of ease. He slowly increased his pace while I started pulling on my tits myself like a woman possessed. I managed to get one tit to my mouth and started sucking on one while yanking on the other like a crazed woman. Daddy Dave liked that; he started going even faster until his lovely cock was hitting the back of my womb with a force that I was having trouble keeping up with. "Don't worry it won't take long now," he whispered as I began sucking, biting and jerking with an intensity that left marks. Dave kept increasing his speed and I could feel my tits shaking like jellies, then he stopped, and with one final thrust, I felt my womb get hotter and hotter as his spunk flooded inside me, I immediately clasped my legs around him, so as not to lose a drop.

Enjoying the moment, I stopped sucking on my titties. So he took over; leaning over me while still inside, he started sucking my boobs until I felt him start to grow inside me again. Very roughly he pulled out, pushed me down on my back and straddled my face then in one fell swoop, put his dick in my mouth hitting the back of my throat. I tried to pull away because it was such a surprise movement, but he held me in place with a hand to the back of my head, making me milk him as he wanked himself into my mouth. He kept going until he began firing jet after jet of hot spunk into my mouth making sure every drop went inside. It was hot, sticky and creamy as it slid down the back of my throat.

Dave slowly withdrew from me as I tried to catch my breath. I started to sit up, but he kept my legs open, "I love to watch my spunk drip out of a freshly fucked cunt," he told me. As I was savoring the taste of his spunk, I felt two of daddy's fingers touch my clitoris, slowly making circles, then he increased his speed, and again, I was panting and groaning as an orgasm tore through my body.

As Daddy Dave gathered his clothes, and got dressed, I lay curled up on the leather sofa, glowing with sexual satisfaction, as I looked at my husband snoring on our bed.

As he left, he gave me deep and sensual kisses, fingering me at the same time. As he ran his hand through my pubes he whispered, "When I fuck you, next time, this will have to go." He gave me one last kiss then winked and exited the room.

∼

I WAS CONSTANTLY, in heat for the whole week of my honeymoon. All I could think about was my wedding night with daddy. Every time Marco and I had sex, I was thinking of my father. Sadly, Marco being Marco, we only had sex three times, each time, very quickly, with him on top. I was desperate to show him my 'new skills', but never had the courage to try, so I had to content myself with masturbation in the bathroom.

I couldn't stop thinking about Dave's 'goodbye' – "When I fuck you, next time", what did that mean?

I got the answer the day after we arrived home, the phone rang, I answered, "Did you have a nice time?" I recognized the voice, it was daddy Dave, my legs turned to jelly, and my heart started thumping, "Yes thanks," I stammered. "Does he know?" He asked, "No, of course not," I whispered. "Has it gone?" was his next question. "Has what gone?" I returned the question, he laughed, "Never mind that, I want to visit this weekend, have you got room for one more?" I got the giggles. "Yes, of course." We made arrangements for his arrival, for the Friday night, his last words were, "Wear your stockings." Then he put the phone down.

∼

MARCO WAS PLEASED that my dad was coming to visit, he and my stepdad had always gotten along well, but I spent my time planning how to get rid of him for a couple of hours!

At 7.30, the door-bell rang. Marco answered; it was daddy Dave. The men shook hands, but Dave kissed me on the lips, and then squeezed my ass. "Good girl, you've got them on!" he commented. I had put my wedding stockings on, under a loose skirt, with a nice fitted blouse, that emphasized my small breasts. When Marco had commented, on my stockings, earlier, I told him that I had a special treat for him later.

After a nice meal and a few drinks, we went into the living room, "Come here and sit next to your daddy," Dave patted the middle cushion on the sofa. I felt my nipples stiffen as I sat between him and Marco.

"Son, you were a bit of a disappointment, on your wedding night," my father told him bluntly. Marco started to make excuses, but daddy wasn't having it. "It's a good thing I was there to take care of my baby girl." I blushed, madly, as Marco looked confused. As Dave looked Marco straight in the eye and never broke contact, he put one arm around me, and stroked my tit, while the other lifted my skirt, exposing the lace top, and stroked my leg; I was helpless, to stop him.

"After seeing your small cock and you passed out drunk, Mia here was not too happy that her wedding night was not going to be all she had imagined it would be. So I decided to service her myself, to stop her from fucking about and being unfaithful to you. Keeping it in the family." Marco began to speak, but my dad continued.

"When you were asleep, I had to give her a proper fucking that a bride deserves on her wedding night." Marco looked shocked, "No, don't thank me, it's what families are for." Dave told him firmly. He began to laugh. "I tell you, if I had known what a sweet piece of ass she was, I would have done it long ago." Marco sat on the other side of me, dumbfounded, unable to speak.

Pushing me by the arm to help me stand up, Dave

commanded me, "Stand up, and show us your panties." Unable to wipe the grin from my face, I jumped up, stood in front of them, lifting my skirt, showing my stockings and transparent undies.

Like connoisseurs, they studied me, "Take the skirt and blouse off," was the next command. Laughing, I unbuttoned the skirt, and kicked it towards Marco, I slowly lifted the blouse over my head, and threw this at Marco, who was now smiling, and I could see his hard on straining against his jeans.

"Come here," Dave said, as he curled his finger, in my direction.

Sexily, I walked toward the only man I had ever called daddy. When I stood in front of him, he ran his fingers over the front of my pants, scratching at my pubes, "I thought so, it's still there. I told you it would have to go, before I would fuck you again." Just like my wedding night the 'dirty talk' was turning me on.

"Marco, get me a towel and hot water, some scissors and your shaving razor." Dave sent my husband out of the room.

My God, he wanted me to shave my pubes! The idea was exciting.

When Marco returned, I was made to take my bra and underwear off, and lie back, over the sofa arm, where they had spread the towel, with my legs wide apart.

They both gathered around, Marco guzzling from a can of beer while Dave set about ready to get rid of my pubic hair. He combed them making them stand proud, then gently began cutting the hair, brushing the loose curls into a dish, "Open wide, we don't want any accidents," he joked. I spread my legs as wide as they would go, exposing my hot end to them. As he trimmed between my legs, he kept telling me 'what a pretty little cunt I had', and 'how stretched it now looked, since he had fucked me'. I was on fire and needed some cock urgently.

When he was satisfied, he produced the shaving brush and after lathering it, rubbed the warm soap all over my private parts, I was squirming, with desire now. Then, with short, careful strokes he glided the razor over the wet stubble, paying special attention, between my legs, slowly, gently, cutting the last of my pubic hair, only leaving a two inch strip, above my clit, it was, to be, my 'porno strip', he said.

"Now, isn't that the cutest cunt that you've ever seen," he asked Marco and he agreed; at this point Marco looked like his cock might explode any moment.

Keeping me in this position, Dave knelt before me, "Watch and learn, this is how you pleasure a woman." He told Marco. He buried his face into my sopping wet hole, and I let out a loud moan, as he ran his tongue along the lips, this was the most fantastic feeling that I had ever experienced, even better than fucking. Dave was lapping at my fanny like a puppy, then flicking my clit, with the tip of his tongue. I was going wild. When he slipped some fingers in, and licked my button at the same time, I howled, as the orgasm ripped through my entire body.

Panting for breath, they pulled me onto the sofa. Dave pushed his fat cock into my pulsating pussy, stretching it, just like on my wedding night. I wrapped my legs around his back, and met each of his thrusts with one of my own. Our bodies were squashed together, as I hung on for dear life while he fucked me. Within a couple of minutes, he was unloading his come into my belly; shaking like a leaf, I needed more cock.

As they changed positions, I looked down at the strip of hair above my clit to see a stream of spunk running out of my hole, and onto the sofa.

Without any ceremony Marco lifted my ankles onto his

shoulders and slid his cock in. He had never taken me like this before and the sheer dirtiness of it all took my breath away. The angle that he was kneeling at was fantastic, for me, as his long thrusts, filled my belly. Dave knelt beside my face, and offered his sticky, spunk-covered cock, for me to suck, I took it willingly. The smell and taste were wonderful, pure sex, obviously he was only semi-hard now, which meant that I could get more into my mouth, and he knew it, as he tried to get it into my throat, as I caressed his big balls.

"Look what you've been missing, boy." Dave laughed at Marco who was now assaulting my tits while he watched me suck my dad's cock for all I was worth.

"Fucking hell Dave, you've stretched her cunt so much, I'm not touching the sides," Marco, light-heartedly moaned, "if I'm going to come I need something tighter than this."

Both men pulled their cocks out, and daddy told Marco to sit on the couch and me to face him straddled on my knees. I complied, holding onto the top of the sofa, and spread my legs with Marco's cock inside me, for better access (or so I thought). Daddy roughly shoved two fingers into my cunt along with Marco's dick, which was soaked with my love juice and his own come, and pulled out some goo. He smeared this between my bum cheeks, concentrating on my other hole. The feeling was quite sensual, as it was the first time that I had ever had this touched. Suddenly, he pushed a finger into my tiny, pucker! Not as nicely as the first time though and he went much deeper this time too.

The sharp pain was wonderful, but it didn't prepare me for what came next. He gently probed the hole with the tip of his cock, then slowly pushed it in. "No! No! No!" I screamed, as the first inch penetrated me, he then pulled it back a little bit, which was just as painful, then in a couple of inches, repeating the exercise, until most of his cock was in my tight, virgin, asshole. After a couple of minutes the pain subsided, my hole was still stinging, but I was stretching to accommodate this long thin cock along with Marco's inside my twat. Daddy's fingers slid underneath, sliding roughly over my button. "Feel that clit, it's as hard as a rock, she loves it, she's soaking!" He shouted to Marco, who joined him, inserting his own fingers in me alongside his dick that was still pumping away. I was rocking backwards and forwards with each stroke, in my ass, as he increased his speed.

As they fingered me a thumb brushed against my clit, sending me into orbit again. As I did this, Dave picked up speed, again, as he was now sliding into my bum with ease. With a huge groan, he gripped my hips, and rammed into me, filling my ass with spunk. When he pulled out, my hole felt as if it was on fire, but it was a wonderful feeling as I felt the come ooze out, onto the sofa and down my legs.

I lay on the sofa, getting my breath back as the men, sat opposite drinking beer, telling me how good I looked, and how 'good' I was. I stroked my freshly shaved pussy, it felt soft, smooth and silky, and was covered with sticky spunk. Theatrically, I ran two fingers from my stretched bum hole, along my swollen cunt, scooping out a load of goo and then licked it off like an ice cream.

We sat around, for the next hour, or so, drinking beer and wine. The rest of the weekend continued in the same vein, with me fucking and sucking, Dave and Marco, together and separately, whenever they wanted me.

When we went for dinner, on the Saturday evening, Dave insisted that I couldn't wear any underwear, which gave them loads of opportunities to feel me up and finger me at dinner, in taxis and bars.

On the Sunday afternoon, while I was sucking his cock one last time, daddy told Marco that, in future, he couldn't have sex with me in the week leading up to his visits, and the night before their arrival, he must shave my pubes, so that I would be 'ready for action'!

After all, it was for his own good, because without my father 'servicing me', I would be out 'fucking strangers'.

THE END
Get Access to over 20 more FREE Erotica Downloads at Shameless Book Deals

Shameless Book Deals is a website that shamelessly brings you the very best erotica at the best prices from the best authors to your inbox every day. Sign up to our newsletter to get access to the daily deals and the Shameless Free Story Archive!

CREAM FOR CARMEN BY LENORE LOVE

Late one night, Carmen hears her widower stepfather weeping downstairs on the living room couch. Touched, she goes to him, only to discover that he's masturbating to memories of her dead mother. Her virgin sensibilities are shocked, but also shamefully curious and, over the course of the next twenty-four hours, she is filled with more hard parental instruction than she can handle.

Cancer took Mom the year before, and so it was just been me and my stepdad in the big old Victorian. I'd been adopted as an infant, so he's the only real dad I've ever known -- which made what happened between us both confusing and yet so darkly exciting.

I had just turned eighteen, and was about three months away from graduating high school. Something awakened me early one Saturday morning, but I didn't know what at first. I rolled over in bed and stared blearily at the clock -- 3:15 AM.

I lay still, listening. My room sits directly above the living room, and sometimes I can hear noises through the floor vents -- my parents having conversations when Mom was alive, or the two of them doing other things the sounds of which made my virgin loins shiver and leak.

I continued listening, and for the first time recognized the sounds for what they were. My father was sitting on the couch directly below me, and he was weeping. Although he'd never shown it, I knew he still grieved for Mom. In some respects, I was still grieving, too.

Oh, I thought dazedly, my heart going out to him. *Oh Dad...*

I thought long and hard about going down to him. I wanted to, but I wasn't sure. Maybe he didn't want me to see him that way -- maybe all I would do was add embarrassment to his suffering. In the end, my love for him won out. Naked, I slid out of bed and slipped into my robe, and then stepped out into the upstairs hallway.

The house was still, cloaked in silence. That pitiful, agonized weeping continued, and I stopped, my eyes widening in the darkness at the top of the stairs. Gooseflesh erupted on my flesh as I stepped forward and put my hand on the railing. I hesitated, took another step forward, and hesitated again.

"Dad?" I whispered.

I didn't need to turn on a light; I knew my around the house perfectly well. I went downstairs, slowly and silently. The couch was at the far side of the living room, past a couple of chairs, the stereo, and the TV. The soft despair grew louder as I drew closer.

"Dad," I whispered. *"Are you all right?"*

It was a stupid question. There was a pause, and then he croaked, "Is that you, Judith?"

I stopped, dumbstruck. He thought I was Mom, or was

pretending to. Did it really matter? All I know is that something clutched my heart and abruptly squeezed forcefully.

"Come to me, baby," he whimpered pitifully.

I couldn't deny the quiet desperation in his voice, but a part of me knew that something wasn't right.

Pale light from a street lamp drifted hazily through the drawn curtains on the picture window, illuminating my father as a mere dark shadow. I crossed the room and sat beside him. Even this close, I could barely make him out, but I could smell the booze he'd been drinking and feel the warmth of his body through his robe.

I reached for his hand in the darkness, but stopped when he put his head against my chest and wept against my bosom. He'd never touched me with so much familiarity, and I tensed immediately. But I also understood what he was feeling right now, and I thought that if resting his head against me offered him some comfort, maybe it might be okay.

I put my arm around him -- when his hip touched mine, I knew he was naked beneath his robe. I stiffened again. I then realized he was pumping his hand steadily between his legs; I heard him moan softly, and I inhaled sharply with shock.

"What're you doing?" I hissed.

His hand continued to pump rhythmically between his legs.

"Remembering you," he whispered.

I just couldn't make sense of it. My daddy was masturbating to some memory of Mom. I was shocked, but I couldn't pull away. His head resting upon my breasts was both frightening and arousing, twin emotions I'd never experienced together. My nipples hardened unbidden beneath my robe in response to this closeness, and I felt myself grow dizzy. I struggled -- he wrapped a big strong arm around me and held me still.

"Please, Judith," he begged softly. *"Just hold me..."*

"No..." I breathed, my heart pounding uncontrollably. *"This isn't right..."*

"Neither was you dying," he whispered, and choked back another sob.

I had no answer for that. Before I could protest, he unwrapped my arm and placed my hand in his lap. My fingers brushed a pulsating rail of blood-infused muscle, and I sucked in my breath, my senses spinning.

"Ahhhhhh..." Dad groaned.

His pulsating member discharged a fire so intense that I simply couldn't grasp the reality of it. I wanted to pull my hand away, but could not. A part of me desperately wanted to see this wonder; another part wanted to flee. My nipples pressing against the inside of my robe felt as swollen as his erection, and I wondered senselessly if he would dare open my robe, press his lips on one, and nibble. My virgin pussy quivered, and I felt a small spurt between my trembling thighs. I moaned when he encircled his shaft with my fingers, and then I gasped, the engorged bellows throbbing and burning in my reluctant grasp.

"Daddy no..."

"Yessss Judith..." he breathed. *"Feeeel how hard I am..."*

Is this what Mom used to do? I couldn't help myself -- prurient excitement surged through me, and I spurted again. He rubbed my thumb upon the spongy softness of his knob, and I felt his oils oozing freely from his slit.

"Oh my!" I gasped.

"Do you like my hard cock...?"

I'd never held one before -- I'd never done anything remotely like this in my life.

"I don't know..."

He exhaled with a loud long groan, the raging engorgement now greased with his wetness as he jacked my fingers up and down its length. God, it felt so huge! I pictured Mom taking this in her pussy or her mouth and couldn't conceive of how she'd done it.

I moaned, shaking. His pubic hair brushed my hand as he guided it below his cock. His balls were hot and heavy and downy-soft, overflowing my trembling, sweaty palm.

"Please stop..." I mewled.

It was a futile request -- I doubted that he even could at this point. And that deep down salacious part of me that capered lewdly in my fantasies didn't really want him to anyhow.

His warm breath in my cleavage was devilishly obscene, but he didn't touch me. I craved his touch, but was consumed by guilt. My excitement knew none of that -- it leaked lubriciously between my legs, and I squirmed. Overcome, I moved my hand back to his cock and gently stroked. His hips bucked involuntarily, and his soft groans intensified in the steamy confines of the room.

"Oh," he gasped suddenly. *"Oh, Judith, don't stop..."*

My tortured psyche was devoured by warring emotions as I helped my father approach his climax. I was aroused and guilty and scared all together. His cock throbbed furiously, a fiery combustion that caused the cauldron of my loins to throb and burn in response.

"Niiiice..." he hissed urgently. *"You always do this so well..."*

Encouraged by his approval, I intensified my strokes, instinctively pressing his bridle with the ball of my thumb. He abruptly drew in his breath and went rigid -- his throbbing shaft contracted powerfully, and a hot sticky mess splooged heavily upon my fingers a moment later.

"Yesssssss..." he cried, hips thrusting. *"Oh Judith babieee..."*

I couldn't believe the force of his orgasm, and my brains reeled impossibly with its unreality. He came and came, dumping hot thick wads like cream from a churn. I imagined my mother being swamped by such a deluge, and my heart thundered so loudly I thought surely he must hear it.

Held captive by my own arousal, I wantonly milked every drop, listening to his ragged breathing as he writhed with my touch. And then I smelled his seed, an incredibly primal scent that twisted every sense I possessed. He leaned close and pressed his lips against my throat.

"It's your turn to cum, Judy..." he murmured, his warm breath horribly intimate. *"I know you want to... I can smell your hot wet cunt..."*

I grew dizzy with lust. The notion that he smelled my leaking pussy was salaciously taboo.

He guided my hand, leaving his resting upon it. Tentatively, I reached between my legs with my semen-clotted fingers and touched my sodden pussy -- could I get pregnant this way? I felt his fingers, too, gently caressing my lips through my wiry dark curls. He tugged gently, and I moaned.

"I've always liked all that hair," he whispered. "My beautiful, beautiful Judith."

My breathing deepened until I could no longer. Waves of bliss lifted me off the couch. He pushed two of his fingers deeply inside and I nearly screamed as a geyser of warm musky liquid squirted loudly across our fingers, thighs, and the sofa. I used my fingers to worry my clit, and another geyser burst forth, and then another as I writhed beside him consumed by my multiples, leaping into a void and falling far beyond the living room...

When I finally returned, I felt my father's lips pressed against my sweaty neck. He was panting softly and quivering.

"Fuck me, Judith..." he whispered.

He slyly slid his hand up my trembling belly and cupped my boob beneath my open robe, gently pinching the nipple between thumb and forefinger. His tongue tickled my earlobe, his breath warm against my cheek -- another delicious bolt of carnality speared my depths, and I squirted helplessly again.

"Nooooo Daddieeee!"

I desperately tore myself from him and fled like a frightened fawn, my face flushed and my bosom heaving. I ran upstairs to my room, slammed the door, and threw myself on my bed, riding a merry-go-round of emotion. That he thought I was Mom had driven my excitement to a level beyond my most prurient fantasies, and that torrid realization only intensified my self-loathing.

Oh my God, I thought again and again. *What have I done?*

∽

I DIDN'T WANT to leave the safety of my bedroom Sunday morning, but I knew I couldn't hide the entire day. That might invite a concerned visit from my dad, and who knew what might happen then. Reluctantly, I dressed and went downstairs.

The delicious smells of frying bacon and toasted bread wafted from the kitchen. I found Dad standing before the stove, preparing to crack four eggs into a cast-iron skillet. He seemed relaxed and content, unlike me. He turned and smiled.

"Morning, Carmy," he said easily.

I cleared my throat, feeling blood rush into my cheeks as I dropped my gaze.

"Morning, Dad."

"You hungry?"

I couldn't believe I had an appetite, but incredibly, I did. I didn't know then that intense sexual exertions could result in one. I nodded, not trusting my voice again.

"Have a seat," he said, and I took one at the counter.

How can he be so at-ease? I wondered.

I kept waiting for him to say something, but he appeared totally disaffected from what had happened last night. It seemed as if he didn't even remember. That might be so, but still... He hadn't been *that* drunk. The memory of what had taken place between us was indelibly seared into *my* mind for all time.

His back faced me, and I studied him closely. He was a tall, imposing man, lean and toned and strong. This morning, he was dressed in black swim trunks and a white tank, the trunks outlining his firm butt and the shirt stretching taut across his shoulders. He was tanned from working outdoors as a contractor, and his brown skin highlighted his thick, silvery hair. My girlfriends talked about him all the time, which I always found embarrassing.

"Sleep well?" he asked.

"I guess."

"That's good. I slept like a rock."

I bet, I thought.

The eggs sizzled and popped. Quickly, he flipped them, tonged the bacon onto paper towels, and pulled two plates from the cupboard. He grabbed a spatula from the utensil drawer and slipped the eggs onto our plates. The bacon followed, along with buttered toast.

When he carried the plates over to the counter, I found myself staring at his crotch. It was the first time I'd ever done it on purpose, and was rewarded with a hefty jiggle in his trunks. What would it be like to see that beast in the light of day? I shivered involuntarily -- whether from excitement or shame I do not know -- and something nasty stirred between my legs.

God, I thought dazedly. *I'm such a pervert!*

He sat down across from me on a bar stool and offered

me a plate. I took it, and his fingers brushed the back of my hand. My heart began to pound.

"I'm walking down to the pond after breakfast," he said casually, his eyes finding mine. "Would you join me?"

I hesitated for a moment. It seemed like an innocent request, but after last night, who knew? All I knew for sure was that to deny him might raise some questions because we'd done this together more times than I could count, even after Mom had passed.

"Sure," I said softly.

He smiled and nodded.

We finished eating. I went upstairs while he cleaned up the kitchen, and dug through my closet for a suit. Normally I wore a two-piece; today, I donned the most conservative one-piece I owned. Still, it clung to me like a second skin, lovingly cupping my pear-shaped bottom, and displaying the top halves of my breasts and the cleavage between. I slipped into a wrap, and shook my head as I fixed myself in the mirror. If things got out of hand like they had last night, it wouldn't matter what I wore.

"I'll be waiting on the porch," he called up. "Grab a couple of towels, would you?"

"Okay."

I joined him on the porch a couple minutes later. He held a beach blanket, so I carried the towels. We started off, walking down the trail through the woods toward the pond. We didn't talk -- there really was no need, and I didn't know what to say anyway. At one point, he took my hand. I don't know why it bothered me -- we'd done this many times, too. I looked up at him, and he smiled. I shivered again.

The trees opened up, and the pond shimmered in the late-morning sunlight. Most of the bank was lined by ferns and cattails, but this spot had been cleared, and sand brought in with a Bobcat. Dad unfolded the blanket and I helped him spread it out.

"Water looks good," he said, and then peeled off his shirt.

I couldn't help but admire him -- even in his late-forties, Dad was in better shape than a lot of the young men at school. His sixer rippled nicely below his toned pecs, the whole covered with a swathe of light brown hair.

"Last one in!" he shouted, and ran into the pond.

He hit the water with a loud splash, submerged, and then exploded through the surface. I put my hand over my mouth and giggled in spite of myself. Maybe it would be all right after all. I ran full tilt and dove into the pond.

The water was cool, but I quickly got used to it. I pushed my head above the surface and found him treading steadily and smiling at me.

"Thanks for coming with," he said.

"Sure."

I studied Dad's dripping features for a moment. Square jaw, bright blue eyes, easy smile, and a sexy dark stubble. When taken as a whole, no wonder my friends gossiped freely behind his back. But when they were around him, they turned into a flock of flustered robins.

Dad and I played in the pond for some time, laughing, spitting and spraying water at each other. I gradually grew comfortable -- now, last night's encounter seemed more like a dream than an actual occurrence. I couldn't have misjudged the situation more wrongfully.

We walked out of the pond and up to the beach. I bent over to pick up a towel, and Dad swatted me on the butt. Not hard, but it sure sounded loud upon my wet suit. I screeched, completely startled, straightened up and turned around fast.

"What was that for?" I exclaimed.

He gripped my shoulders in his strong callused hands and stared me straight in the eye.

"That's for being a naughty, naughty girl, young lady."

I felt like a doe caught in the headlights of an onrushing car, frozen to the spot and totally unnerved. My mouth went dry and my heart began to pound. I licked my lips, and said --

"I don't know what you mean..."

I knew perfectly well, of course. He cleared his throat.

"I'm talking about last night, Carmen."

"That was --"

He shook his head, cutting me off. I hoped he would say that it had been wrong, that we couldn't do anything like that again, and even though the pleasure we'd experienced had been great, it also had been sinful and shameful and morally corrupt. Instead, he said --

"Do you love me, baby?"

That took me by surprise.

"Of course, I do," I croaked.

His hands caressed my shoulders, his eyes piercing, frighteningly intent.

"How do you love me?"

I didn't know what he meant. I shook my head, trying to clear it. Finally, I replied,

"Like a daughter...?"

His fingers idly toyed with my suit straps. He drew in a breath and pursed his lips, and I trembled so hard I thought my joints might pop.

"That's not what I want, Carmy."

The sun had grown obscenely hot on my flesh.

"What... what do you --?"

"I want you to love me like a wife."

Before I could respond, he slipped the straps off my shoulders and peeled the top half of my suit down to my waist. He did it so quickly, I was caught completely flat-footed. My breasts tumbled free, my wet nipples swelling immediately from the breeze, and he devoured them greedily with his eyes. Dazedly, I watched him put his hands on them and cup, running his thumbs gently across my swollen areolas.

"So beautiful," he murmured, gazing openly. "I've always admired them."

"Daddy please..." I whimpered.

He continued to caress and stroke until I literally lost my breath, my entire body trembling and my heart pounding. And then, without even waiting to be asked, he cocked his head, leaned forward, and engulfed my left boob with an open-mouthed grunt of satisfaction.

"Daddiieeee!" I gasped, but I didn't push him away.

Instead, I reflexively held his head, running my fingers through his hair as he feasted upon my flesh, shame and excitement flooding me as they had last night. I moaned helplessly, his tongue a slippery serpent winding its way upon my hardened nipple, driving little sparks of pleasure through my bosom.

Something abruptly prodded my lower abdomen. I looked down between us and inhaled sharply. A terrific bar of muscle stretched his trunks to their limits at a ninety-degree angle, the end of which now pushed insistently just above my mound. I nearly fainted.

"Tastieee..." my dad crooned, slurping my other boob like a bowl of whipped cream.

He pushed a hand between my thighs and probed firmly through my suit. I felt his index finger sink in just a titch, and my clitty shrieked urgently. I squirted like a whore, and he chuckled lewdly when he felt my juices soak the fabric.

"God, you get wet..." he muttered.

His lips left my tits, traveled upward across my jaw, finally landing on *my* lips and pressing hungrily. His tongue danced with mine for a moment, and every dirty thought or urge I'd ever experienced now sucked me down like a whirlpool. I moaned wantonly, slipping my arms around his waist and crushing him close, wriggling my virgin loins upon his throbbing member.

Oh God... I thought mindlessly. *Oh God oh God oh God...*

He broke off the kiss and stepped back. Staring at me, he grasped his tented trunks and stroked. I couldn't help myself -- I reached forward and put my hand on his.

"*Show it to me, Dad...*" I hissed. "*Pleezee show it to meee...*"

"*Show me yours first...*" he commanded.

I hesitated for a moment, knowing that everything about this situation was completely unacceptable. But as long as we didn't go all the way, was it *really* that bad?

I peeled my suit down to my ankles and stepped out of it, staring at him challengingly. His eyes widened as he beheld my naked body in all it's creamy splendor.

"*Oh...*" he muttered. "*Jesus, that's nice...*" He pointed at the blanket. "Lie down and spread your legs. I want to see your pussy."

I hesitated again, this time from embarrassment. Mom had seen my vagina, of course, when she'd shown me how to use a tampon. But this was so completely different. I wasn't on my period, and this was my dad. And, to tell the truth, I've always thought my pussy seems kind of ugly compared to my girlfriends. My pink lips are a little loose and puckered, and the inside looks somewhat red and meaty.

"What's the matter?" my dad asked, snapping me back to reality.

I told him, and he touched my cheek.

"You let me be the judge of that, baby."

And so, I lay on the blanket and tentatively spread my legs. His eyes burned a hole through my hairy crotch, and he licked his lips.

"Wider," he commanded.

Heart pounding, I did as I was told, my face burning with embarrassment and shame.

"Carmy," he breathed. "You're beautiful."

My heart pounded even harder, and a chill consumed me.

"Oh Dad..." I murmured.

He stroked himself through his trunks, and vented a tiny grunt. A large wet spot appeared where his knob pressed against the fabric, and I thought immediately that he had climaxed.

"Did you just cum, Dad?"

"No."

"Then show me. You promised."

My dad peeled his trunks to his ankles and kicked them aside. My eyes widened like saucers, full of fearful disbelief.

He was big, all right, bigger than most of the men I'd seen on the Net. His glistening pink member jutted forth from his stubbled groin like the handle on a handsledge, a little narrow at first and then widening steadily to the head. The terrible pulsing shaft wore a roadmap of tiny blue veins, with a thick one on top and another down under, all of it capped by an immense, shiny, red heart-shaped helmet that gleamed lubriciously in the sunlight. His testicles, which had drawn up tight against his body, seemed almost anti-climatic by comparison.

He groaned and stroked his juicy cock again; the slit smiled at me and an oily string seeped forth and dangled precariously.

"Jesus Dad..." I whispered.

"Play with your pussy..." he hissed. *"I wanna see you squirt..."*

Tentatively, I put a hand on my vulva and rubbed. A jolt of pleasure rocked my loins, and I moaned softly. My cunt lips ballooned with blood, growing loose and flappy, and my fingers squelched in the wetness.

"Jesus..." Dad hissed.

I continued wantonly, now lost in perversion. I frigged myself as I had on so many other nights, inserting fingers and worrying my clit, my eyes never leaving his. He stood over me, stroking slowly and steadily, his mouth ajar and his gaze almost stuporous. Another jolt rocked me; I bucked my hips and juice poured forth, splashing against my fingers and spraying every which way. I cried out, shaking, and squirted again.

"God-damn..." Dad grunted.

He straddled my tummy and dropped to his knees, cradling his puling cock between my tits. He oiled my cleavage, and then lewdly rubbed back and forth.

"Squeeze your titties together..."

I did as I was told, enjoying the burning hardness between my breasts, his knob not even an inch from my mouth. He slimed my flesh, the squishing sounds slick and moist, and then bucked his hips forward and pushed his knob against my closed lips. He pushed harder, forcing my mouth open around his glans. I snorted, my jaw tendons popping upon its mammoth roundness and my wide eyes watering.

"Ohhhhh fuuuckkk meeee..." he gasped.

I struggled, gagging as his sticky oils filled my mouth. Finally, out of desperation, I nipped his knob, and he drew back with a roar.

"What the fuck, Carmy!"

"You're hurting me, Dad!"

He was instantly consumed by remorse. I could see it twist his face, and my heart raced out to him.

"Oh Daddy," I breathed. "I thought we were just playing together. Anything else would be just wrong."

He remained silent, starting at me. I reached out and put my hand on the beast, trying to completely encircle it and so woefully unable. The muscular pink truncheon surged in my palm, and my dad groaned gutturally.

"That's right, baby," I murmured, my heart pounding with anticipation. "I wanna see you shoot..."

He put his hand on mine and we stroked together, from the base of his shaft to the heights of his flaming knob. Back and forth, steadily and repeatedly. His body quaked, his thighs squeezing my sides, my full titties bouncing with our movements. He abruptly braced himself on his hands and knees and earnestly rubbed against my tummy, breathing heavily and sweating in the late-morning heat. I stared down past my breasts and watched, waiting for the explosion.

"Uhhhhhhhhhh..." he grunted.

"Daddy --"

He stiffened, grunted again, and then howled like a dog, his knobslit flexing. I cried out joyfully, a creamy blast suddenly splattering my belly. He fired again, a torrent splooging across my tits. I grabbed his cock and held it, marveling over the incredible contractions as he fired again and again, a final forceful load slapping my chin, lips, and nose. He collapsed on top of me, our bodies puddled with his seed.

It took him a long moment to catch his breath, during which I could feel his semen dripping down my cheeks. I squirmed beneath him, disgusted.

"Dad, I feel gross..."

"Shhhhh..." he hushed.

And then, amazingly, he licked his cum off my face. The intimacy I experienced with him at that moment, the closeness, was indescribable. I desperately wanted to kiss him again, and I did, wrapping my arms and legs around him and furiously crushing my lips upon his. We held each other for a moment, and then he stood up and extended a hand.

"Let's clean up," he said softly.

We went to the pond and washed each other, playing and giggling like kids. Finished, we returned to the blanket, dried each other off, and lay down. Again, I was overwhelmed with emotion. I clung to his lean, muscular body and whimpered like a child. He stroked my hair like he had when I was little, and I sighed with contentment.

"Any regrets?" he asked softly.

I lifted my head and met his gaze. "No."

"Good."

"Dad?"

"Yes?"

"Why did you call me Mom's name last night?"

He paused for a moment. "I don't know."

I thought that he did, but I wasn't going to press him further. My fingers wandered idly down his ridged stomach to grasp and fondle his heavy, flaccid organ. I felt him for a moment, squeezing and petting, and then giggled when he twitched.

"What?" he grunted.

"I was just wondering how long it takes to get hard again."

"Let's find out..."

He rolled me onto my back and leveraged his body above me. He leaned down and began kissing me, starting with my mouth and working his way slowly down my body, across my breasts, where he paused for long moments, and then my tummy. He tongued my navel exquisitely, and then moved lower. He rubbed his nose in my pubic hair, his breath warm on my pussy lips. I suddenly realized what he intended to do.

"No, Dad, it wouldn't be right."

"But it would please me, Carmy, and get me *soooo haarrrd...*"

Without waiting for my reply, he flicked his tongue across my quivering wet lips, sending a shockwave through my loins. I jerked, stunned by its power. He chuckled, and flicked me again.

"God, you smell sooooo gooood..." he breathed.

He abruptly spread my legs wide and plunged his tongue into my depths, slurping and smacking like a pig at a trough, uttering little grunts of pleasure and blowing tiny bubbles. Riotous desire swept through me; I grabbed his head and held him fast, undulating my steamy snatch against his face, smearing him with juice. He tongued my clitty while inserting a finger, and then two, exploring methodically, and I writhed like a trailer park slut, consumed by blissful prurience.

I heard him grunt when he encountered my hymen. He looked up, his face dripping wet and amazed.

"Really?" he asked.

I nodded dumbly, unable to speak.

"We'll take care of that right now."

He stabbed me with his fingers. Pain lanced through me, and I cried out. He immediately soothed me with his tongue -- at first I was disgusted that he was certainly slurping my blood, and then I was filled with excitement so great that I grew dizzy with joy. My orgasm immediately roared forth, overcoming the pain, twisting my loins and limbs as I sprayed his face. He gargled, drinking deeply, and I sprayed him again.

He quickly rose to his knees between my spread legs and roughly pulled me to him by gripping under my knees. The beast had been reborn, I saw, and he now popped its head on my pussy with a moist *splat!* I writhed, my shame and pleasure perversely combined.

"Nooo Daddieeeee...!"

He either didn't hear me or he just plain ignored my entreaty. Either way, I squirmed licentiously as he chunneled his fat hoggish length back and forth upon my bloated lips.

"Noooo Daddieee we can't...!"

He grunted unmindfully. He grasped his cock and knob-popped me again, and then again and again, bouncing his glans on my clitty until I helplessly cried out and squirted once more. He prodded my portal with that bulbous appendage, slipping its tautness just past my entrance. My eyes widened with both shock and awe as I realized the wondrous sensation of his entry.

"Noooo Daddieeee I'm not on the pill...!"

He obviously didn't care. He pushed further, both of us staring between my legs as the beast slowly disappeared through my matted dark jungle and entered its tight squelching lair.

My senses spun deliriously -- viscerally captured by lust and depravity and beautiful immorality. Helplessly, I humped my hips against him, sinking additional inches, until suddenly, shockingly, he bottomed out against my cervix, still with several more inches to go.

I can't begin to describe the sensation. I was lifted out of myself on a cloud of wanton bliss, climaxing furiously with a spray around his pole. He grunted lasciviously and thrust, spearing my cervix again. He pulled out and thrust, pulled out and thrust, the feeling so shocking and crude in my virgin pussy that I could only mindlessly wail and go along for the ride. Sloppy wet squelchings accompanied our rutting as he fucked me like his whore, long and hard and deep, rocking my body and flopping my tits. My body was sheened with greasy sweat, my hair matted tangles. His face was wracked by a savage purpose, and I watched rivulets of sweat trickle down the slab of his chest.

I had already orgasmed multiple times -- I knew he must be close.

"Don't cum in meeee Daddieee....!"

It was like begging some natural force not to fulfill its

destiny. He stiffened, sucked in his breath, and then slammed home with all his might, pinning me helplessly beneath his weight. His throbbing cock contracted, filling my tortured depths with his globs of seed. They cannonaded against my cervix, and then squished out around his poling meatus and drenched the crack of my trembling rump. The sensation was so joyously naughty that I howled like a crazy woman and climaxed with him.

He pulled out and rolled aside, his seed and my juices clinging in pearly strings to his organ. I whimpered, and threw myself across him. Mom had been one lucky woman.

"Didn't you hear?" I demanded softly, licking his nipple. "I'm not on the pill."

"I don't care," he murmured. "Do you -- really?"

"No," I said breathlessly, suddenly realizing it was true. "I don't anymore."

He smiled wearily and kissed me. "Do you suppose we made a baby?"

I sighed. "I don't care about that, either, right now."

He chuckled. "Just what *do* you care about, baby?"

I grasped his slippery sodden organ and squeezed, giggling when he winced.

"How long will it take *this* time, Daddy?"

THE END
Get Access to over 20 more FREE Erotica Downloads at Shameless Book Deals

Shameless Book Deals is a website that shamelessly brings you the very best erotica at the best prices from the best authors to your inbox every day. Sign up to our newsletter to get access to the daily deals and the Shameless Free Story Archive!

WHAT LAURIE DESERVES BY PHILLIPA SAINT

If you ask Laurie what she deserves, she'll tell you 'everything', and that she won't settle for less.
If you ask anyone else, they'll tell you she's a spoiled brat whose arrogance pushes away everyone around her.
But some people can't simply be pushed around, and one afternoon she pushes her stepfather too far. And he'll not only teach her a few hard lessons, he'll give her everything she REALLY deserves…

Laurie parked her car more or less in the center of the underground lot. She glanced around, checking to see if anyone else was near. There wasn't, so she focused on Josh, leaning over and kissing him. He kissed her back, hard, his tongue searching hers and tasting it in just the right way.

He was a good kisser, she'd give him that.

She broke the kiss and reached for his pants, undoing both his belt and his zipper before he could react.

His cock sprang out, pointing straight at the top of the car. It was smooth and hard, and one of Josh's best features. Maybe *the* best.

"Whoa," he managed to let out as she grabbed it. His head turned to all sides furiously. "What if someone sees us?" He asked it like they had never done that before.

"Relax," she said as he did just that, his body responding to her rubbing by melting into the car seat. "No one can see it from outside. It's not like you have that big a dick."

He laughed. "Bitch."

"You love it."

"Yeah. Yeah, I do," he said, sounding like he meant it.

Laurie checked the parking lot again out of the corner of her eye. There was still no one around.

She felt some ambivalence towards that. On the one hand, the perspective of getting caught jacking off her… well, boyfriend was too strong, but her whatever-Josh-was… She liked that feeling. A lot. On the other hand, if she was going to get caught, she'd rather it didn't happen while she was doing something as lame as a hand-job.

"God, that's good," Josh said. "Faster. Do it faster."

"Like that?"

"Yeaaah…"

It was amazing. There was something about giving hand-jobs that seemed almost magical to Laurie. As hard as the cock was in her hand, the man itself completely melted. She loved the feeling of control that gave her.

Josh's hand reached for her leg. She didn't react. The hand went further up her leg. She still didn't react.

Then it reached her crotch. And she let go of his cock.

"Okay, no. That's it."

"Come on…"

"Oh, suddenly you're not afraid to get caught?" She

crossed her arms under her breasts, accidentally brushing against her still hard nipples.

"It'd be worth getting caught. Come on…"

"I said no, Josh. You know the rules."

He sighed. His rod visibly became less of a rod, and more of a deflating rubber staff. "I don't get this. Are you saving yourself for marriage, is that it?"

She scoffed. "No. I'm saving myself for someone who deserves it. I'm not gonna fuck someone just because."

"What the fuck, Laurie! What do you mean, I don't deserve it?"

"Do you? What did you do to deserve my virginity, Josh? All we do is go to the movies and hand-jobs in the car."

"That's all you want to do!"

"Then you should surprise me," she said with a shrug.

"Oh, for— Well, if I don't deserve you, why the fuck are you still with me?"

She paused, not answering, and smiled. Leaning over, she kissed him on the lips, keeping them closed so as not to let his tongue in. She caressed his face with as much tenderness as she could muster.

"Oh, Josh. Honey. You really don't know?"

He smiled, but not one of his full, happy smiles. This was more expectant, maybe even suspicious.

"Tell me," he said.

"I'm still with you…" Her hand reached for his cock, and it instantly stiffened again.

"Yeah?"

"Because no one better has come along yet."

His eyes widened, his smile disappeared. He shoved her hand away from his cock as he put it back in his pants.

"Well, fuck off, Laurie! What the fuck? You're a bitch, you know that? For real."

"Yet you're still here," she said with an almost childish smile.

"I can fix that right now." He shoved open the car door, jumped outside and violently threw the door back to close it, then walked away without even looking back over his shoulder. "Go to hell, Laurie."

"Josh, don't be stupid. I can drop you off at home."

He screamed, his voice echoing across the parking lot.

"Go fuck yourself, Laurie. And delete my number. Forget I even exist."

He did say something else, but by that point she'd closed the window and turned the engine back on, revving it up just to drown out his words.

In truth, she never had his number. He'd given it to her, true, but they only talked via messaging app. And of course, his contact would soon be deleted, which amounted to the same thing.

As to forgetting him… Maybe she would. Whenever she counted the boys she had been involved with, she was always under the impression she was missing one or two. Not that there had been that many, but they simply hadn't been that memorable. Josh certainly wasn't. Maybe he'd be the one to be permanently forgotten.

Her friend Tori once asked her how she expected them to ever be memorable if she refused to sleep with them. "Hell," she had said, "at least blow them once or twice. That should give you a couple of interesting memories."

To Laurie, it was exactly the opposite. They'd have to be memorable BEFORE they took her virginity. Not because of it. She deserved no less.

As she drove past Josh and he flipped her the bird, she knew that he definitely deserved to be forgotten. And in short order, she was sure, he'd get what he deserved.

"What's wrong with the one you have now?" Adam asked.

Laurie glared at her stepdad. He was sitting on one end of the dinner table, so no more than a few inches away from her. Like he had for almost two years, ever since he moved in with her and her mom Emily.

It still didn't feel like he belonged at their table.

Laurie turned to her mother. "My car is old, Mom. I can practically feel people just looking at me when I'm driving. Like, look at that loser with that crappy car."

"Laurie, no one cares about your car, and you know it." Emily kept her eyes on her plate of spaghetti, but she had stopped eating.

"Moooooom, come on, I need a new one. Can I have one? Please?"

Adam sighed. "You're almost nineteen, Laurie. Why do you insist on acting like you're nine?"

She turned to him again, grinning. "Nice of you to remember my age, Adam. But I wasn't talking to you."

Emily shouted before Adam could say anything. "Stop that! We're all sitting at this table together, and we're all family."

"Says you."

"Laurie!" Emily threw down her fork so hard Laurie thought her plate had broken. "Apologize at once."

"No."

"It's fine," said Adam. "I know how she gets. Let her have her tantrum, maybe she'll get more rational later." He paused, then glared at. "In a decade or two."

"No, it's not fine. You're her stepfather, you put the food on the table just as much as I do, and she needs to learn to respect you once and for all."

"I respect him," Laurie said. "Like I do anyone. Even

homeless people on the street. Besides, that's not the point. Why can't I have my car? I know you can afford it, Mom."

"I could, but I'm not rich and I won't spend money on your every whim."

Time to pull out the big guns, Laurie thought.

"Dad would give me a new car."

"Not if he cared for you, he wouldn't. But sure, go ahead and ask him."

"What's the point?" Laurie sighed. "You'd just call him and tell him not to give it to me. It's not fair."

"That's right, I would. And I would even if you actually deserved a new car, which you keep proving you don't. Want a new car? Get a job and buy one. And if you don't like that, well, you have your car now. Use it or lose it."

"If it was up to me," Adam said, "you wouldn't even have that one anymore."

"Except it's not up to you, Adam. You're not my father. And I'm glad."

"Laurie!" shouted Emily.

"You know what?" Laurie continued. "I think you're glad you're not my dad too. I've seen the way you stare at me when Mom isn't looking."

"What the f—" Adam let out.

"Do you even know the man you've married, Mom?"

"All right, that's enough!" Emily shouted as she jumped from her seat and stretched out her hand. "Hand them over."

"What?" Laurie asked, puzzled.

"Your car keys. Your car privileges have just been revoked. Hand them over."

Laurie's jaw dropped. Emily was dead serious, waiting with her hand out. Adam watched them with a smug look on his face.

"I'm nineteen!"

"So?" said Emily.

"So, it's my car!"

"If you need a new one, then this one is obviously no use to you. So hand over the keys."

"But how will I get anywhere?"

"You're catching on. Good. Give me the keys, now!"

Laurie's eyes jumped from one side of the table to the other, from her mother to her stepfather. Neither was going to change their mind. Laurie figured she'd lost the battle, and her eyes dropped towards the table.

"They're upstairs."

"Then you'll go get them after dinner."

"Fine."

They finished the meal in silence. When they were done, Emily followed Laurie to her room, and Laurie handed her the keys without a word. Emily left the room and Laurie locked the door behind her, then threw herself on her bed, her mind racing.

The battle had been lost, but there was always another day. She'd keep fighting for what she deserved. She'd get it, too.

Her thoughts drifted to Adam. She hadn't lied when she said she'd noticed him looking. Which was only normal, she supposed. Men usually did, and she had to admit, Adam was a man too. But while the others didn't bother disguising their looks, Adam always made the effort to look away.

If Laurie was being honest, she'd stared at him herself a few times. He was certainly nice to look at.

She pictured him in her mind, as vividly as she could, and felt flush, blood rushing to her face and other, more intimate parts of her body. She instantly tried thinking of something else.

Except… Why should she? He was a man. She was a woman, and she knew that in spite of what he said, he knew how much of a woman. Why shouldn't she think of him like that? Yes, he was her stepdad. But the more she thought of it, the more she felt her body respond in ways it seldom did to other men.

Her hand went into her pants, and inside her panties. She was even wetter than she'd realized. She took her hand out, took off her pants, then ran her fingers over her pussy lips, getting them wet and sticky. She brought them to her mouth as she replaced one hand with the other, touching herself as she sucked her own moistness out of her fingers. Enjoying the taste and the feel of her pussy while she finger-fucking herself.

She heard steps passing her hall. It was probably Adam, he usually went to bed around that time, to read for a while before Emily joined him.

Laurie went for her clit, working it perfectly. She almost moaned, but held silent.

As Adam's steps grew farther away, she cursed herself for holding back. What would he have done if he had heard her pleasuring herself? Would he have stopped and listened? Would he have gotten hard, and rushed away to jerk himself off?

In that very moment, something inside her exploded, making her whole body convulse with pleasure, the sensation rippling all over her body seemingly forever.

Then forever ended, and she stretched back on her bed, gasping.

Tomorrow was another day, indeed.

And one day soon, all three of them would get what they deserved.

∼

Laurie stretched in the lounge chair by the pool, enjoying the feel of the mid-afternoon sun on her skin. It wouldn't give her a tan, but it felt nice enough. She had slept in until one, and had only just left her room. Consequently, she still didn't feel fully awake, and the soft sun lulled her into a comforting, dreamlike state.

She'd chosen the smallest bikini suit she had, barely more than three patches of strategically placed fabric connected with string. Not something she would normally wear at home, but she had decided to change that.

Instead, she'd just not wear it when her mother was home.

Emily had left for work early, as she usually did, so Laurie had missed her entirely that day. As she had Adam, in fact.

But Adam should be coming home soon.

By Laurie's account, that was his weekly afternoon off. Laurie wasn't normally home at that time, but she knew from both him and her mother that he enjoyed relaxing by the pool. And she figured she'd keep him company that day.

She laughed, weirdly nervous. Some small part of her conscience reminded her that Adam was her mother's husband. Her stepfather. She shouldn't do what she was planning on doing.

The rest of her was delighted and eager.

Besides, it wouldn't be that big a deal. She would tease him a bit, just to get back at him. And, admittedly, for the thrill of it. But it would never get far enough to matter.

She heard the front door open and close not long after that. Instinctively, she turned on the chair, facing upwards, stretched her arms by her sides, and arched her back just enough to accentuate her breasts without making her uncomfortable.

Then she closed her eyes, and waited.

She didn't have to wait long. Bare feet stomped from inside the house, getting closer. She heard the glass door to the pool yard open, then close… Then the steps stopped.

"Oh," Adam said.

Laurie had to hold back a smile.

She opened her eyes, and languidly raised her head to look at him.

"Ah, you're home," she said.

His eyes were locked on her, exactly as she had intended.

What she hadn't intended, however, was the impact that seeing him had on her.

He was wearing only a tight speedo, leaving nothing to the imagination. Clearly, he expected to be alone.

And something moved inside the speedo. Something big, and growing.

Laurie could feel her own body react to him. Her nipples hardened, forcing themselves against the fabric of her bikini. She hoped Adam noticed.

But she could always improve the odds.

With one smooth motion, she untied the string behind her back and removed the bikini top, exposing her breasts to the sun, and to her stepfather.

The bulge in his pants grew bigger and fatter.

"What are you doing, Laurie?"

"Getting rid of my tan line." She turned over slightly, pointing her nipples at him. "How does it look?"

"Like you're asking for trouble," he said as he moved over to the other side of the pool, and laid down on a lounge chair directly in front of her. He flexed his leg, raising his knee to partially hide his erection, but he wasn't very successful. "Yesterday you accuse me of looking at you inappropriately, and now you pull this shit? Why don't you save it for your boyfriends?"

"No, I said I caught you looking at me. Not that it's inappropriate, or that I don't like it. And they don't deserve me."

"Any of them? You're trying to tell me, what, you've never..."

"No, I've never. Is that so hard to believe?"

"Frankly, yes."

"Well, that's your problem. I haven't found a boy that deserves me yet."

She got up and went around the pool, sashaying towards Adam. He tried looking away. And soon failed, his head turning back to her, going all over her body before landing back on her breasts. Yes, he could see her pert nipples, all right. And he was enjoying it, too.

"And what?" He asked as she sat down in the chair right next to his. "You're trying to convince me you think I deserve you somehow? You hate my guts, Laurie. And frankly, I'm not that fond of you either."

"I like you fine. Besides, they're all… boys. You? You're…" Her eyes landed on his hard-on. She didn't try to hide it. Neither did he. "You're a man."

"And you're a brat. A sexy brat, I'll admit that much, but still a brat."

"You're funny."

"And you're my stepdaughter. Remember that."

She giggled, and pulled her chair closer to his, then bending over to whisper close to him.

"I know that… *you* know that…" She reached for his crotch, and grabbed his dick. "But this doesn't."

He recoiled, and tried to pull her hand away. But he didn't try that hard, and instead of letting go, she started rubbing it over the fabric of his speedo. Within two strokes, his purple head was peeking out.

"Oh, God," he moaned. Why did men always get religious about hand-jobs? "We shouldn't be doing this."

"But you want me to, don't you? Because I do. I really, really do."

"Do you?"

"Yes."

He pulled his cock out of his speedo, letting it tremble in the open air. Laurie grabbed it again, and rubbed faster.

"Do you, you brat?"

"Yes…"

He sat up from his chair and put his hand at the back of her head, catching her by surprise. But she didn't resist, and he pulled her hard against him as she kept rubbing him. They kissed hard, his tongue pushing itself between her lips, and she accepted it eagerly. He was passionate, vigorous. Hungry for her.

And Laurie was starting to feel the same way about him.

"Oh, wow," she said when they finally broke off the kiss, his hand still at the back of her head. "Adam, that was—"

"Shut up, you brat."

"What?"

"Shut the fuck up. You wanna get what you deserve?"

This was getting out of hand. All Laurie intended was to tease Adam a little, to push him far enough to embarrass him. That was it. But she had gotten physical, and now things were going too far. She needed to stop it. Before they did something they would both really regret.

"Yes, sir," she told him. "I do."

"Yeah?"

"Yes."

"Then do as you're told. Come here."

He pulled her out of her seat, then pushed her forward and towards his lap. For a second she feared he was going to impale her there and then, but instead, he bent her over his lap. And before she could say anything, he slapped her butt. Hard.

"Ow!"

"You had this coming, you brat."

Laurie was going to get up and leave. But she couldn't.

It wasn't that he was holding her down. He had one hand keeping her in place, yes, but there was no actual force in it.

No. What kept her down was the ass slap. It hurt. He was rough on her, and it hurt a lot.

But it shook something inside her. It reverberated through her body, a jolt of electricity coursing through her whole body.

And it made her pussy quiver with delight.

Another slap, even harder, on the same cheek.

Laurie moaned.

A third one.

"Oh, God," she said. She was the one getting religious now, and it felt entirely justified.

"Is this what you deserve, brat?"

"Yes, sir."

"And you deserve even more. You want even more punishment, don't you?"

"I do. Punish me, Adam. I want more."

She didn't even know what she was saying anymore. All she knew was, whatever he wanted, she would agree to. She was too far gone to care.

"Not Adam, brat. You call me sir and nothing else."

He slapped her again, this time on the other cheek.

Laurie's body quaked. It felt like all her blood was going in three directions. To her head, making her dizzy and lightheaded. To her butt cheeks, making them swollen and probably red. And to her pussy, making her dripping wet.

"Yes, sir."

"Oh, look," Adam said. "You're drenched." He grabbed her thong and pulled it out of her, exposing her ass and pussy to him. She didn't care. "Are you enjoying this, brat? Are you enjoying your punishment?"

"No, sir."

"Yes, you are. Look at this." He rubbed his finger across

her pussy, getting it sticky with her juices. At that moment, she wanted to suck his finger more than anything in the world. "Your cunt is soaked. You are enjoying this a little too much."

Laurie didn't know what to say anymore. Finding the right response required thinking, and she was way beyond that.

"Do you want me to punish you more?"

"Yes, sir. Please."

He pushed her off his lap, and it was all Laurie could do to keep from falling down.

"You're not getting it. If you're enjoying it, it's not punishment, is it?"

She didn't know what to say to that, so she just stared at her feet, suddenly embarrassed.

"Get on your knees," he said as he removed his speedo. She obeyed as fast as she could, which considering she was still dizzy, it wasn't all that fast.

Adam held his own hard-on in front of her, and her eyes locked on it.

His cock looked even more steel hard than before, and Laurie wondered how that was even possible.

"You say you're still a virgin," he asked. Laurie nodded. "Well, is your mouth still virgin too? I'm sure you must do something to those boys you go out with."

She shook her head. "I mostly give them hand-jobs. But no, my mouth isn't— I've done that. Yes, sir."

In truth, she had only given one blow-job, to a guy two or three exes ago. Laurie didn't enjoy it all that much. But maybe she just wasn't used to it.

Still. She wanted to blow Adam. Her mouth craved his cock, the thought of him sticking it between her lips practically made her drool.

But she didn't want to seem too eager, or too inexperienced. Either could make Adam change his mind, and she was not going to risk that.

"Then let's see how good you are," he said, positioning himself in front of her.

Laurie adjusted herself so her mouth was lined up with his dick. She reached out to his cock with her hand first, and saw it trembling. She was actually nervous, and hoped he wouldn't notice.

"Ow. Stroke it, brat. Don't crush it."

"Sorry, sir." She took a gentler touch to it, and instinctively kissed his tip as she stroked. It jumped at the touch of her lips, like it'd been electrified.

Laurie liked that, and had to restrain a smile.

Since he wasn't giving her any further instructions, she decided to stop stroking, holding his cock by its base just to aim it at her mouth. But instead of inserting it, she felt the need to lick it first, gentle tongue teasers along the sides and at the tip.

Adam moaned.

She kept doing it, until she was sure every inch of it had been licked at least twice. Laurie found she liked the taste of it, and despite her previous bad experience, was now definitely eager to suck him off.

"Am I doing this right, sir?"

"Passable," he said. "Keep going."

She licked it once more, and then decided to stop waiting and wrapped her lips around the glans. For a brief moment, she wondered what she should do next, and decided to suck at the tip for a bit.

His body shook. Yeah, he liked that.

Slowly, she took more and more of it in, all the while holding the shaft at the base. He felt bigger in her mouth than he did in her hand. Was he actually swelling, or did it just feel different?

Didn't matter. All she cared about was his taste, how good it felt in her tongue, how she liked the feeling of his hard cock filling her mouth as she fucked his cock with her lips.

Adam didn't move, letting her control her own pace as she moved back and forth on his rod.

She didn't take him all the way in. His cock was just too big, all she could do comfortably was getting halfway down his shaft. But she felt she was doing it right, and from the way his body trembled, it seemed she was right. She was certainly enjoying herself.

Then he grabbed her head and stopped her moving.

"Stop. Hold still." She did, but kept his cock in her mouth. He grabbed the sides of her head.

"Do. Not. Move."

Laurie knew what he was about to do. She feared she wouldn't be able to take it. But Adam didn't want her to move, and she would do her very best to do as she was told.

He slowly pushed himself inside her mouth. She let him, keeping her lips as tight around his shaft as she was able. He was more than halfway in, past what she had been able to take in before, but he kept going. It was uncomfortable, yes, but it also felt good. The feeling of her whole mouth full like that, her limits stretched… She liked that. She liked that a lot.

His tip reached her throat, and she gagged. He pulled back, taking it out as Laurie composed herself.

"Were you going to puke on my cock, brat?"

"No. No, I wasn't, I swear, it was just a reflex."

"Yeah. Yeah, I should've known you wouldn't be able to handle it. But that's okay. We'll work on that."

Laurie parted her lips, ready to get her mouth fucked again.

"No, no, no. We're done with that for now."

Laurie whimpered. She wanted more. She wanted him to

fuck her mouth until she could take it all in, and he'd come down her throat...

But the way he said it, he made it sound like there would be a next time. That was definitely something to look forward to.

He picked her up by her arm, more gentle than she would have expected, and directed her toward the chair.

"Lie down on that."

She tried, but she was so uncoordinated she almost tripped and fell. He guided her by the arm, and once she was on her back, he pushed her legs apart, exposing her wet cunt to him.

The touch of her buttocks on the fabric hurt. Laurie wondered how she was going to be able to sit down for the next few days.

But in front of her, standing tall, was her stepfather Adam, cock in hand, gazing at her pussy.

Every other consideration was pointless.

She reached towards her clit, tentatively. He didn't say anything, so she started touching herself.

"Are you going to fuck me, sir?"

"I might. But I get the feeling that you want that, you slutty brat. So that's no punishment, is it?"

"No, sir. I'd really not like that at all. Of course it would be punishment. And I deserve it. I deserve it so much. Please punish me, sir."

"Yeah? You want me to punish you with my cock?"

"Mm-hm." She bit her lips, trying to contain the rising pressure inside of her. If she was going to come, she did not want it to happen before her virginity was gone.

"All right. I'm going to stick it into your pussy, and come inside of you. That'll teach you."

He bent over and got on top of her, his hard rod rubbing against her dripping pussy. The lounge chair creaked from their combined weight, and Laurie wondered if it could handle the repeated motion about to test it.

Adam must have thought the same thing.

"Yeah, this is no good," he said as he got back on his feet.

Laurie sat up. "What?"

He held out his hand to her. She took it. He pulled her up. Then, before she could react, he pushed her into the swimming pool.

Laurie shrieked as the shock of the cold hit her warm body. He'd pushed her into the shallow end, and at that point the water only got up to her hips, so even with the splash she barely got wet above the waist. Still, the cold threatened to take away her excitement.

Then Adam jumped into the pool right next to her, and with one motion took her arm, spun her around, then pushed her against the edge of the pool. Instinctively, she bent over, and he approached her from behind.

"Yeah," he said as he put the tip of his cock right at the edge of her cunt. "You want me to go in?"

"Yes."

"Are you sure? Are you positive you want me to take your virginity?"

"Yes."

"What if I come inside you and you get pregnant, brat? What then?"

"God, I don't care. Just fucking do it. Please, sir…"

Her voice barely raised above a whimper. He tried and failed to suppress a laugh. Then she felt him push in, and nothing else mattered.

She had expected him to push himself hard into her. To not care if her first time would hurt or not. Instead, he didn't so much push as press himself inside, with no rush at all. The feeling sent shivers all over her body, both from excitement and anticipation. Her hymen had been broken by her first dildo a long time ago, but this was her first actual cock, and she was as anxious for it to fill it as she was worried if it would hurt her.

It didn't. Quite the contrary. Her pussy fit around his hard flesh as if it had been molded for it. At that moment, if he'd asked, Laurie would've sworn it had.

Her body quaked with every inch he conquered. Then, an eternity and an instant after he first went in, his hips were against hers, his cock fully inside her.

"No way you're a virgin. I slid right in."

"I am. I swear I am, sir."

"Not anymore, you're not."

"I was."

"You're lying. And you know what that means."

"I need to be punished?"

"Damn right."

He slapped her ass hard, making her shriek, and at the same time he pulled himself out then thrust himself back in hard. The sensations combined and made Laurie's entire body tremble.

Adam pushed himself inside her again and again, fucking her faster with each movement. Laurie could barely feel the water temperature anymore. All she could feel was that man's rod filling her, touching her inside where no one had touched her before, taking her pleasure for his own. Making her his fuck toy.

Then, amidst all the mental noise that was all her mind was able to produce, one thing he said came back to her. 'What if I get you pregnant?'

There was no conscious thought as an answer. She was unable to think, just feel. And what she felt was a sudden terror at the thought of her belly swelling, of a baby growing inside her.

But above and beyond that was an excitement at the

thought of his cum inside of her, swimming all the way up, and hitting a target nothing else could. Of claiming her as his in a way that nothing else could match.

And suddenly, the pressure inside her rose beyond all resistance, and she exploded. Electricity rippled inside of her, like every cell in her body screaming all at once as he kept fucking her hard and fast with no protection.

Laurie screamed again and again, her body convulsing uncontrollably.

"Yeah, that's it," he said. "Come, you slutty brat. Come for me."

And maybe as a reaction to her body shaking, maybe because he wanted her to ride out her orgasm, Adam slowed down for a moment.

"No," she said between gritted teeth, as her hand reached out to his hip and pulled at him. "More. Fuck me more. Just. Keep. FUCKING ME!"

And for once, he was the one that did as he was told. He fucked her even harder than before, his every thrust reverberating inside her, making her pleasure just go on forever and ever. His grunts and moans mixed with her screams of delight as the water splashed around them.

The image of Emily coming in then, catching her daughter and her husband fucking in her pool appeared in Laurie's mind, and it just made want to be punished even more.

And having seemingly read her mind, Adam reached for her hair, bundled it and pulled it hard with one hand as the other held on to her waist and his hips kept pushing hard into her. The nerves under her scalp lit up, mixing in with her pleasure, sending her over another threshold, and she screamed so hard she was afraid someone would hear her.

Inside her quivering pussy, Adam's cock seemed to swell, and he grunted louder and thrust faster, and within seconds she could feel slick jets of something squirting inside her. And slowly, as her own pleasure finally subsided, so did Adam's thrusts. She looked over her shoulder as he pulled out of her. He looked tired, but he was smiling. She turned around, her face to the late afternoon sun. He climbed out of the pool and laid on the floor next to her. They didn't speak or touch for what seemed like a long time.

Finally, he got up from the floor. Laurie opened her eyes and saw him once again stretch out his hand to her.

"Are you gonna throw me back in the pool?"

He smiled and shook his head. She took his hand, and he helped her up.

"So," she said. "What now?"

"What do you mean, what now? You played with fire, you got burnt."

"And getting burnt was my punishment, is that it?"

"Yep. You said you wanted what you deserved. You got it, missy."

"So… This only happened because I deserved it, is that it?"

"What are you getting at, Laurie?"

She grinned, then slapped him hard across the cheek. She doubted she'd actually hurt him, but he was slack-jawed nonetheless.

"Also, I hate your guts, and I wish Mom had never married you, and you're a disgusting human being."

Laurie could see the anger rise behind his eyes.

"What the fuck—"

"Do I deserve more punishment now, sir?"

The anger dissolved. He smiled.

Then, as she deserved, he punished her some more.

THE END

Get Access to over 20 more FREE Erotica Downloads at Shameless Book Deals

Shameless Book Deals is a website that shamelessly brings you the very best erotica at the best prices from the best authors to your inbox every day. Sign up to our newsletter to get access to the daily deals and the Shameless Free Story Archive!

KEVIN'S KISSES BY SAFFRON SANDS

Millie was never happy having to share Kevin. So when she finally gets the man of the house all to herself, Millie finds herself pleasantly surprised at just how much attention Kevin is eager to give her.

My heart pounded in my chest as Kevin entered the room. It happened all the time now. I wasn't the only one who found my stepfather attractive, so did all my friends. Bethany was the worst. It had gotten so bad that I had to end our friendship when I noticed that she had somehow managed to catch my daddy's eye.

I was curvier than my girlfriends and never really expected to be more than Kevin's special girl, but when my mom walked out the door on my eighteenth birthday, I found myself to be more excited than sad.

Neither Kevin nor I were especially shocked or saddened by my mother's departure. We sat on opposite end of the sofa and watched her carry a suitcase to the door.

"I don't expect either of you to understand." She said as she stood in the doorway.

Kevin and I looked at one another then back to my mother. I tried but couldn't think of anything to say. My mom had never been the nurturing type. I couldn't think of one instance she had actually been there for me. As I thought about it, the truth was I actually more stunned that she managed to stay in my life until I hit eighteen, than I was that she was walking out the door.

We both stared in silence. My mom exhaled loudly then pulled the door shut behind her.

Kevin cleared his throat and leaned back on the sofa. I looked over to see a furrowed brow. He was obviously thinking, but he remained quiet.

I cleared my throat and he looked over at me. "Umm, are you okay?" he asked.

I nodded. "Yeah, I'm good. You?" I asked.

Kevin nodded. "Yeah." He smiled awkwardly, then put his face in his hands.

At first I thought he was going to cry but then I realized he was trying to cover up that he was laughing.

"I'm sorry, Millie." He looked over at me with a concerned expression.

I smiled weakly. "You don't have to be sorry. You didn't do anything wrong." I said.

Kevin moved close to me, wrapped his arm around my shoulders and pulled me close. "You didn't do anything wrong either. This is all on your mom. Don't ever think it had anything to do with you."

I snuggled in against my stepfather's chest. I was at my happiest when we were alone. I smiled and inhaled his scent. Now I would have him to myself all the time. "Thanks, Daddy."

Daddy kissed the top of my head. "I love you." He said.

"I love you too." I replied.

~

"So she just packed a bag and left?" Clara asked her eyes wide in disbelief.

"Yeah. Daddy and I were just sitting on the sofa. Next thing we know, mom is standing in the doorway with a suitcase." I said.

"How are you handling it?" Clara asked.

"I'm fine. I mean it is weird that she is gone, but she never really acted like a mom." I said. "How many men has she gone through? As a child, I never even knew who would be at my house when I got home from school." I chuckled.

"So Kevin is letting you stay?" Clara seemed shocked.

I looked at her with a puzzled look. "Why wouldn't Daddy let me stay?" I replied a little snottier than I had meant to.

Clara shook her head. "It is so weird you call him Daddy." She sighed out loud and shook her head.

"Why?" I asked.

"Well he's actually your stepfather for one, and also it's just freaking creepy. You're too big to be calling a grown man Daddy." She said and shuddered as if she were repulsed.

"Well I like calling him Daddy and he likes it when I call him Daddy." I stood and picked up my backpack.

Clara giggled. "I bet he does."

I looked down at her. "And what does that mean?"

Clara looked up at me. "Oh come on, Millie. Everyone knows how much you love your Daddy." She rolled her eyes. "I bet that is why your mother left. No one likes being the third wheel."

I felt my face redden. I was so mad I wanted to punch

Clara. I nearly blurted out some obscenities, but changed my mind. I just shook my head at her, turned and left.

I slammed the front door and marched straight to my bedroom. I slammed the bedroom door and tossed myself on the bed. Before I knew it, tears were streaming down my red hot cheeks. I'd never been so angry in my life. Who was Clara or anyone else to judge me? Besides, they were wrong. Nothing was going on between me and Daddy.

"Millie?" I heard Daddy crack my bedroom door. "You okay?" he asked.

I buried my face in my pillow to hide my now red and puffy eyes. "I'm fine." I replied, my voice muffled by the pillow.

"You don't sound fine." He said and sat on the edge of my bed.

My heart fluttered when I felt his hand on my lower back. He slowly caressed me as he tried to soothe me.

I didn't know what to do. I froze. My body stiffened at his touch. "I'm fine." I said. "Or I will be fine." I mumbled and lifted my face from my pillow. "I just had a fight with Clara."

"I see. Well, I'm sure you gals will sort it out." Kevin said as he continued caressing my back. "You want to talk about it?"

I did, but I couldn't. How could I? There was no way I could just blurt out how I felt about him. "No. It will all work out." I said.

Kevin patted my behind. "Well how about you freshen up and we go do something fun?"

I nearly squealed when he gently slapped my bottom. "No, thanks." I said. "I think I'd rather stay home."

"Well, we can do something here then? Pizza and movies? Fire up the PS4?" he chuckled.

"Maybe another night." I sniffled and wiped the tears from my cheek.

"Okay." Daddy said. "Let me know if you change your mind." He said as he walked out of my room.

"I will, Daddy." I looked over my shoulder and forced a smile on my face. "Thanks."

"Anytime, Sweetie." He said and pulled the door closed.

∾

It had been nearly a month since my mother had left. Daddy and I quickly fell into a routine. He got home from work to a home cooked meal I had cooked for him. We watch television, discussed our days, and then went to bed.

Tonight I noticed Daddy acting stranger than usual. He was fidgety and when I would catch him looking my way he would suddenly drop his glance to avoid eye contact.

Daddy ate his dinner in a hurry, picked up his plate and put it in the dishwasher.

"Everything okay?" I asked when he returned to the dining room. "Was the food not good?"

Daddy nervously cleared his throat before speaking. "It was delicious as usual." He brushed some crumbs from the table to the floor. "I'm just feeling kind of off tonight." He said. "I think I'm going to go to bed a little early."

"Are you sick?" I asked suddenly concerned.

"No." Daddy waved his hand and shook his head. "Nothing like that. Just tired I suppose." He chuckled nervously. "I probably just need to get some extra sleep." He said then waved at me. "So ummm…goodnight." He said.

I stared at him as he turned and walked away. "Good night." I replied not sure what was going on.

After cleaning up dinner, I decided I may as well get comfortable and watch a show. I slipped into my favorite oversized sleep shorts and pulled on a thin T-shirt. I figured since Daddy was already in bed covering my dark nipples wasn't really something I had to worry about tonight.

I plopped down on the sofa and put on one of my favorite shows. Before too long, my eyelids got heavy and I was lying down on the sofa. The next thing I knew, Daddy was kneeling on the floor beside me, his hand dangerously close to my crotch.

I suppressed a squeal as I woke up. Daddy was staring between my legs, his finger lifting the hem of my shorts as he peered under the material.

I closed my eyes not wanting him to know I was awake. My heart pounded in my chest, and my pussy fluttered with anticipation. It took all I had to not make a sound.

The flickering light of the television was the only light in the room. I tried to peek through squinted eyes to see Daddy but I quickly closed my eyes again too chicken he would notice I was awake.

I could hear his breathing was fast and shallow then I heard him growl.

I couldn't resist a quick look. I opened one eye to see Daddy was stroking himself.

I closed my eyes tight and involuntarily moved my hips. I couldn't help it. My pussy was aching now. All I wanted was for Daddy to touch me.

I was worried Daddy would leave, but he didn't. He was quiet for a few moments then his fast breathing started up once more.

I couldn't stand it. My body tingled and I needed to be touched. I moaned softly and stretched as casually as I could. I heard Daddy move as I rolled over and repositioned myself on the sofa. I now faced the back of the couch so that Daddy could no longer see my face. My knees were pulled up in a fetal position, my legs slightly parted giving easy access to my now wet slit should Daddy be brave enough touch it.

I heard him mumble under his breath, but I couldn't make out the words. After a few more moments, I felt the heat of his hand and the material of my shorts being tugged on.

Another mumble I couldn't decipher and his finger dragged along the moist cotton of my panties.

I couldn't help myself and I instinctively jutted my behind toward him giving him even better access to my throbbing pussy lips.

"Mmmm." I whimpered as his finger lingered over my clit. Daddy applied a slight amount of pressure then made little circles with the tip of his finger around my pulsating nub.

He whispered something as he caressed along the elastic of my panties then slipped his finger under the now soaking wet material.

I suppressed a moan as his finger made contact with my flesh and I felt my panties being pulled aside. His finger now moved along my slit. He paused over my clit for a moment then moved his finger down to my pussy hole. I felt my walls contracting as his finger lingered. I couldn't see his face but I just knew he was contemplating whether or not he should dip his finger inside me.

I swallowed hard as I waited. My body ached and I had never longed to be touched more than right now. At last I felt the tip of his finger part my labia. Slowly he slipped his finger inside me.

I heard him gasp and I couldn't hold back a deep throated moan.

His finger all the way inside me Daddy froze once more. I shuddered and felt my walls contracting around his digit.

Daddy groaned as my pussy continued to flutter then I felt him pulling out of me. I thought he was going to stop and I wanted to cry out but he didn't pull all the way out, he added another finger and plunged them both deep inside me.

"Oh!" I couldn't help it. Daddy's fingers felt so good. I arched my back and pressed my buttocks back toward him.

I kept my eyes closed and he continued to finger me from behind.

I listened to the sound his fingers made squishing in and out of me, and I was certain I could also hear the sound of him jerking his meat.

Daddy slipped his middle and ring finger inside me. His index finger now flicked rhythmically over my clit.

Another moan escaped me but there was no way I could suppress my sounds of delight now. I was going to climax and there was just no hiding it. I emitted a soft squeal and my legs clamped tightly together as I came.

Daddy let out a grunt and I knew he had come too.

We both lie there softly panting, his fingers still inside me as my pussy convulsed around his fingers, as I listened to Daddy's breathing.

I was too afraid to let him see that I was awake even though there was no way Daddy didn't know I was. Instead, I lay there as he slipped his fingers from my hot pussy.

Daddy stayed a moment longer before I heard him getting up. Still lying there, eyes closed I faked being asleep as he hovered over me.

"I love you." He whispered then kissed my head.

I wanted to respond, but didn't dare. Daddy pulled the blanket from the back of the sofa and draped it over me. I listened as Daddy walked down the hall until I heard his door close. Eyes still shut tight, I stayed on the sofa until I fell back to sleep.

∽

Needless to say, breakfast the next morning was more than a little awkward.

Daddy poured two glasses of juice, set one before me then quickly returned to the refrigerator. "Scrambled eggs okay?" he asked as he placed the carton of eggs on the counter.

"Sounds good." I said. "Should I make toast?" I started to get up but Daddy quickly motioned for me to stay at the table.

"I got it." He said rather hurriedly.

I jumped when the sound of the frying pan clanged onto the stovetop. "I can help." I said but Daddy declined any assistance.

I watched as he fumbled around the kitchen. Normally he was shirtless with baggy pajama pants, but this morning he wore a shirt and robe. I had to admit he looked rather uncomfortable concealed under all that unnecessary clothing. I looked down at my own attire. I was still wearing my pj's from last night. I let out a gasp. No wonder Daddy was avoiding me. My dark areolas were plain as day through the thin cotton of my shirt.

I got up and quickly made my way to the bathroom. I looked in the mirror. Yep. You could see my nipples big time. I put on my bathrobe and returned to the kitchen table.

Daddy handed me a plate and I could see that he was relieved that I had covered up. I thanked him for my food. We sat eating in silence and I couldn't help but wonder whether he were wearing his robe to cover an erection.

"How did you sleep? Are you feeling rested today?" I asked and Daddy nearly sprayed orange juice from his nose.

After a brief coughing fit, he finally said "I slept just fine." He didn't look at me instead he pushed his eggs around on his plate. "Umm, how about you?"

"Fine." I said as I buttered a piece of toast. "I sleep pretty solid." I added as I recalled having quite erotic dreams of Daddy and I. "I even had some very interesting dreams." I immediately regretted saying that and looked down at my plate. "Anyway, I hope you were able to get lots of rest." If I could kick myself, I would have but instead I just told myself to stop talking.

"Yeah, I did." Daddy said and got up from the table. "I'll be working late tonight then going out with the guys after." He said as he put his plate in the sink. "Don't feel like you have to wait up for me."

I felt my heart sink in my chest. Was Daddy regretting last night? "Okay." I said and watched him leave the kitchen.

After breakfast, I walked down the hall to my room. I paused outside of Daddy's door. I knocked but he didn't answer. Slowly I turned the knob and peeked inside. I didn't see Daddy, but I could hear the shower water was still running.

My heart pounded as I pushed the door open and I stepped into his room. The bathroom door was cracked. My mouth went dry and my pussy tingled at the thought of seeing him naked.

I mustered up the courage to walk to the cracked door. Slowly I peered through the crack. I could see the steam from the hot water swirling in the room. The mirror was fogged and I couldn't make out his reflection. I thought about stepping just inside to see if I could see him through the shower door but the water shut off and Daddy stepped out of the shower.

I suppressed a gasp as he stood naked, water dripping down his back and over his muscular buttocks. I could see just a flash of his cock as he reached for a towel. I wanted to stay and watch but I feared being caught so I rushed out of his room and gently pulled the door shut.

Once in my room, I collapsed on the bed. My body was on fire with the desire for his touch. I couldn't push the thought of our little taboo episode last night, or how my dreams had taken things even further.

I closed my eyes and ran my hand over my mound. I pictured Daddy naked, on top of me, his cock pressed against my virgin slit as I begged him to pop my cherry and fill me with his seed.

My hand slipped under my panties. I massaged my clit like Daddy had while I pretended to be sleeping on the couch. It felt good but not near as good as when Daddy did it.

I continued playing with myself for a few moments but my sexy thoughts were suddenly disrupted at the notion of seducing him tonight. Then I remembered that he was working late and I would be in bed when he came home. I was sad for a moment but then the idea struck me. I would be in bed when Daddy came home, but there would be no way he could resist touching me when he discovered me naked and on display.

~

IT WAS after dark as I sat on the sofa anxiously waiting to put my plan into action.

I had been so nervous I couldn't even eat my supper. Instead, I sat before the television nibbling on crackers and sipping an herbal tea that claimed to calm your nerves.

I looked at the clock. Ten Thirty. Daddy wasn't much of a night owl and should be home anytime now.

I turned off the television and went to the bathroom to brush my teeth. I stared in the mirror, my robe opened enough that I could see my bare breasts. I had never really been overly confident in my body since I was curvier than most of my friends, but tonight I felt sexy. I pulled my robe wide open and gazed down at the tuft of muff hair between my legs. I stroked the thick patch of curls and a ripple of gooseflesh rushed over me. "It won't be long now." I smiled nervously and walked to my room.

I left my bedroom door cracked wide enough that Daddy would be able to easily see inside as he made his way to his room. And to be sure that I directed his attention my way, I turned on the rope of purple lights that hung around the ceiling of my bedroom. The light was soft but there was enough that Daddy would be able to see that I was naked and sprawled out on my bed.

Lying there quietly I waited and listened to hear Daddy enter the house.

It took longer than I had anticipated for Daddy to come home. I was actually about to lose my courage, when I heard the sound of his keys hit the table in the entryway.

I strategically draped the sheet over my midsection, one arm at my side the other up by my head. I parted my legs, left leg straightened my right leg bent all to give Daddy a good view of my pussy should he decide to enter my room.

My heart pounded as his footsteps got closer. I heard his steps stop and the sound of my bedroom door opening wider.

I could barely hold still. I felt so vulnerable knowing he was standing in the doorway looking at me. I wanted to open my eyes but dared not.

I could hear Daddy move closer. His breathing quickening as he stood at the foot of my bed.

"Millie?" I heard him whisper, but I didn't move a muscle. "Baby, are you awake?" he whispered again but I remained still.

I listened as Daddy moved to the side of my bed. Next, I felt the mattress sink as he slowly sat on the edge. "My God." He mumbled and I felt the small bit of sheet that covered my abdomen slip off me.

I was completely naked before him. Totally vulnerable

and hoping that Daddy would not be able to resist taking the opportunity before him. In my mind I screamed for him to touch me, but to my surprise I felt the mattress move again, this time Daddy was getting up.

I nearly opened my eyes but thankfully I didn't. I heard Daddy's zipper then the sound of his pants hitting the floor. A soft moan escaped my lips and I hoped that didn't frighten him away. I was relieved when I felt his weight return to the mattress. I wondered if he was naked as he scooted close to me. That is when I felt it. Daddy's cock brushed against my left hand. I wanted to hold it but that would give me away so I remained still as he slowly positioned himself beside me.

His breath tickled my ear and I turned my head to the side. I didn't want him to look at my face and see that I was only pretending to be asleep.

His nose nuzzled my hair and I heard him inhale my scent. I felt the tip of his finger teasing my left nipple that made me tremble and caused my nipples to grow even stiffer than they already were.

He rolled my rouge nub between his finger and thumb then softly pinched it before pulling away. I heard him lick his fingers then he rolled my nipple some more making something deep in my core flutter.

It was all I could do not to moan or sigh at his touch. My pussy ached more than it ever had and I wondered if it were possible to come from nipple stimulation as my moisture pooled between my legs. I wanted Daddy's touch so bad but he continued to play with my nipples. I decided I had to make a move. I licked my lips, moaned softly, and gently placed my hand closer to his cock.

Daddy gasped and I felt his dick twitch. He pressed his cock to my hand and I felt something wet and sticky smear on my flesh.

I held still and waited to see what he would do next and

what he did shocked me. He touched himself then touched my lips. I could smell the musky scent of whatever sticky substance from his cock as he spread it along my bottom lip. I licked my lips softly brushing his fingertip as I tasted the saltiness of his manhood.

Daddy pulled his hand away and softly ran his finger along my slit.

I involuntarily gasped and wiggled at his touch as Daddy covered his finger in my wetness and then it happened. Daddy spread his finger along my lip then pressed his finger inside my mouth. There was no way I could continue to pretend I was not aware of what was happening.

My eyes opened as I sucked Daddy's finger, tasting my own juices as he moved in close to me and kissed me hard.

"Mmmm" I moaned as his tongue darted in and out of my mouth alongside his finger. My chin was instantly covered in a mixture of our saliva and my pussy juices. When our kiss broke I realized I was now holding his thick cock in my hand.

"Oh, Millie." Daddy said and pulled me to him. "I have to have you." He said and pushed me to my back as he positioned himself between my legs.

I stared in shock as he scooted down and gripped my thighs before taking my pussy in his mouth. "Oh!" I bucked my hips and wiggled in his grip. "Oh Daddy!" I cried out at the overwhelming sensation of his warm mouth on my hot pussy.

I heard muffled groans as he continued to lick my pussy, his tongue rhythmically lapped up my juices then flicked my tiny little clit before he stiffened his tongue and pressed in as deep in my hole as he could.

All I could do was flop like a fish out of water as he continued to pleasure my pussy in ways I had never even imagined. Suddenly, my back arched and my body stiffened as the most intense tingling sensation spread over me and my pussy exploded with intense pleasure.

Daddy grabbed my sheet and wiped his face as I lay gasping for air. He pulled me toward him and placed his cock to my tight opening and that is when panic struck.

I placed my hand up to his chest and blurted out "I'm a virgin." between gasps for air and waves of my continuing orgasm.

Daddy smiled and rubbed the head of his cock along my slit. "You've never been with a man?" he asked as he teased my clit with the tip of his dick.

I shook my head. "Never."

"You want me to take your virginity?" he asked.

I nodded without hesitation. "Yes."

"Ask me." he grinned and put the head of his cock at my opening and parted my labia with his thickness. "Ask me to fuck you. Beg me to fill you with my come."

I licked my lips as my pussy fluttered in anticipation of his manhood filling me. "Fuck me." I whispered. "Fuck me, Daddy." I added as I stared up at him.

I could tell he liked that so I repeated it as I lifted my hips to him. "Fuck me, Daddy." I said and bit my lower lip.

Daddy gnashed his teeth as he pressed his cock a little deeper. I could feel him trembling as he slowly inched his way inside me until he met some resistance. "Your pussy is so hot. So tight." He groaned as he lowered himself on top of me.

I wrapped my arms under his and clung to his shoulders as his hot breath tickled my neck. "You ready for Daddy?" he asked in a low growl.

"Yes." I whispered and closed my eyes as Daddy thrust his hips forward and popped my cherry. My body stiffened as the pain shot through me.

"Mmmm." Daddy groaned as he kissed my neck and

gently nibbled at my sensitive flesh. "Relax and the pleasure will quickly wash away the pain." He said as he pushed his groin to me and slowly pressed his pelvic bone to mine.

He was right. The pleasure of him pressing my mound while his cock massaged my sensitive pussy walls made me nearly instantly forget the sharp pain of being a virgin.

His pace quickened and I knew he wouldn't last much longer. The thought of his seed spilling inside me sent another ripple of pleasure through me and I found myself lifting my hips to his, meeting his rhythm, and grinding my pussy to him in the hopes of taking every inch of his thick cock.

"Oh Daddy!" I clawed at his shoulders and wrapped my legs around his hips. "Oh Daddy!" I cried out again as I felt him twitching inside me.

Daddy let out a loud growl then gripped my hips as he thrust hard and deep inside me. "Oh, God!" he grunted and collapsed on top of me. I cried out as I felt the first rush of hot semen released inside me. Daddy groaned again as he thrust his hips and another hot load was deposited deep inside.

Daddy remained on top of me. The hot sticky mixture of our sex oozed from my contracting pussy and trickled down my cheeks to my bedsheets.

When he rolled off me, he pulled me to him and I snuggled in close. His lips pressed to my head and he gave me a kiss then I heard him sigh.

"Daddy?" I said.

"Yeah?" he replied.

"What we did..." I wasn't sure what to say what I wanted to say. "Clara says it's not right." I continued.

"This is none of Clara's business." Daddy said. "Besides, I've tasted you and I can't give you up now." He kissed my head then my nose.

I thought about how much I loved feeling Daddy inside me, and a shiver rippled through me as I thought of him coming inside my unprotected pussy. "I don't ever want to give you up either." I nuzzled his neck with my nose.

"Mmm…should I fill you up again?" Daddy said and pulled me on top of him. "You look good up there." He massaged my breasts then ran his hands along my sides before resting them on my hips. "I can't wait to see the curve of your belly when I knock you up." He lifted his hips to me, and I felt his cock stiffening.

I probably should have been shocked by his comment, but I wasn't. I was turned on at the thought of my belly swelling with his child and my pussy ached with need.

THE END
Get Access to over 20 more FREE Erotica Downloads at Shameless Book Deals

Shameless Book Deals is a website that shamelessly brings you the very best erotica at the best prices from the best authors to your inbox every day. Sign up to our newsletter to get access to the daily deals and the Shameless Free Story Archive!

IN HIS BAD BOOKS BY STEPH BROTHERS

Luscious brat Billie has a little hero worship going on with the man of the house. She likes pleasing him, and hates when she's in his bad books.

Angus is a sci-fi novelist, with a sharp mind and an even sharper tongue. He's the strong, silent type, especially when he's working in his office.

But when this brazen brat sneaks in and snoops on his computer, she finds the story he's working on is nothing like sci-fi at all. It's dirty, filthy smut, complete with hot spanking. She's even more shocked when she realizes the main characters are clearly based on Angus…and herself.

When the man himself gets home and busts her, wet-handed, things come to a head. And he expects her to take the same kind of punishment as the heroine in his story.

Suddenly, being…in his bad books…is not such a terrible thing.

I so very rarely had the house to myself these days, even now that mom had walked out on us. But the place was absolutely silent as I got out of bed.

For a moment, I listened carefully, hearing nothing at all that would tell me daddy was home. He's not my actual dad, but he'd been in my life for nearly 7 years now. He was pretty much the real deal.

I bit my lip as I considered heading down to the kitchen, exactly as I was. *Naked*.

But there was every chance daddy *was* here, and just being quiet. Not for the first time, I wondered if it would please him, to see me naked. It was my favorite thing to do. Please daddy.

But in the end, I slipped on the shorts and blouse I'd worn yesterday. I didn't bother with bra and panties.

See, my stepfather works from home, as a novelist. The fact he could come up with whole stories just from inside his head was amazing to me.

He only wrote boring old science fiction that would put me in a coma, but I still had more than a little awe about the whole process. Plus, he made enough from it that he didn't need a day job.

All that meant, though, was that he was home pretty much all the time. Don't get me wrong. I sure didn't mind spending time in his company. He was kind of my dream guy. Tall, strong, handsome and intelligent. And he actually gave a damn about me as a person, unlike the horny boys back at school.

I was only 12 when he married mom, and I'd planned to be the bitch from hell to my new stepfather. Instead, I'd sort of fallen in love with him right from the start. Well, maybe not love, but just the sight of him did make me warm in all kinds of nice places.

But it was when I turned 18 that my mom decided being a wife and mother was the most boring thing on the planet, and she headed off into the sunset with most of their shared bank account.

That was almost a year ago, now, and it was kind of weird. Not that she was gone. No, the weird part was that neither of us seemed to miss her at all. She'd clocked off from this family long before she ever left it.

Now, with me a few months out of school, I'd been hanging around home more than ever. I needed to get a job sometime soon, but as a C student with double Ds, the only place in our little town I was qualified to work was the local strip club. Some might say I was overqualified.

Overqualified, but completely inexperienced. I mean, I knew what effect my body had on the boys—and men—in town. A girl would have to be deaf and blind not to notice the slobbering and cat-calling.

But where all my friends had handed out their cherries like free samples at the supermarket, I'd held onto mine. I had only one special customer I wanted to give it to.

Daddy.

If only I could somehow make him notice me as a woman, instead of as his stepdaughter. But he locked himself away in the study for hours on end, working away on his epic stories. I barely knew if he was home or not half the time.

That was why I'd taken to checking out porn on my laptop. And *that* was why daddy had confiscated all my electronics. Even my cellphone.

I walked silently up to the door of the study, wondering if daddy was working in there. If he was out, like I suspected, then I figured I could bring up a little dirty action, grind one out at record speed, and get the hell out again.

And if he was in there? Well, maybe that could work in my favor, too.

There was a note on the door.

Billie. Had to go to the store. Back at ten.

KEEP OUT!

Angus

I wasn't convinced he was out of the house. He'd been known to put up notes like that just to keep anyone from interrupting his work.

So, I tapped on the door in case he was waiting in there. When there was no reply, I crept inside.

His computer was clearly still on, but in sleep mode. Keeping an ear out for his truck returning, I moved the mouse and his password screen came up.

He's a very smart man, but he's always underestimated just how devious I can be. I broke his code last month. It took me all of seven seconds.

I sat on his chair and flinched at the movement I saw off to the side. Then relaxed as I realized it was my reflection in the tall mirror he'd mounted on the wall there. He said it was so he could make the faces of his characters, and then describe them.

When my heart rate settled again, I typed in the password. My birthdate, of all things. Maybe he thought that was just something that would never occur to me.

When the screen came up, I rolled my eyes. He'd left one of his silly story files open.

Fearing I'd die of boredom, I reached for the mouse to close the document. But then I noticed a couple of words in it.

Dirty words.

The kind you wouldn't usually find in a sprawling science fiction novel. At least, not so many of them in a single page.

I paused with the mouse pointer over the *close* button, as I scanned a little more of daddy's story. There were lots of *cocks* and *pussies* and *fucks* and all the kinds of words he still frowned at me for using.

"Holy fuck!" I couldn't contain my shock. *My stepdaddy was writing porn!*

I bit into my bottom lip and listened hard, making sure he hadn't arrived home. Satisfied I was still alone, I scrolled back to the start of the story.

When I read the title, I had to suppress a giggle. *Dirty Dungeon Brat by Jenny Tools.*

My laughter dried up, along with my mouth, as I scanned his words. It started out innocent enough. A young woman named Bambi—*god, really?*—had been locked in a dungeon for treason.

It moved along quickly enough, with her getting a few choice punishments at the hands of the oafish guards.

Daddy's descriptions really hit home for me. Especially the mentions of how Bambi's ass went so red when the guards whipped it. While her wrists were bound in steel chains.

Things turned even more interesting when the broad-shouldered freedom fighter, Gustave, arrived, and broke her out. And then proceeded to punish her in his own, delicious ways.

My breath raced as I read through his detailed descriptions of Gustave's body. His hard-muscled body, and his soft-lipped smile. Tattoo of a leopard on his chest. And dark brown eyes that filled young Bambi with all kinds of sinful desires.

"You're not the only one, Bambi my girl," I murmured. Suddenly I was wishing Gustave was real, and right here with me. He sounded fucking perfect. From his glistening muscles, to his flowing dark hair. From his smoldering eyes, all the way down to his big cock.

I'd watched a little porn, of course. I'd read a few dirty stories, too. But knowing that these words came from my stepdaddy's mind made them hotter than anything.

Feeling more daring than ever, I unbuttoned my shorts and slid a hand down inside. The heat of daddy's words had lit a short fuse inside me, and I desperately needed to work my way through it.

I could barely move my eyes fast enough to drink in the story. He began to describe young Bambi's naked form, and it was clear daddy had a real thing for this girl.

He spared no inch of her luscious body, from her long, golden-blonde hair, to her pretty sky-blue eyes, to her pouty mouth. Her slender neck and full breasts, her soft, round belly with a small scar above the navel, and her tightly-cropped bush.

As I ground at my clit, reading the blow by blow account of the handsome Gustave taking the comely Bambi, my body quivered with desire, and my hair fell in front of my eyes.

Wait…

My *long, golden-blonde hair*…fell in front of my *sky-blue eyes*.

Fuck! And Gustave had a tattoo of a leopard on his chest.
Just like daddy's.

Bambi and Gustave…were *Billie and Angus*.

"Oh, holy hell."

Daddy had not just been writing filthy stories. He'd made *us* the main characters, and was living out all his wildest fantasies through them.

And given how juiced up my pussy was, he'd clearly written *my* wildest fantasies, too.

I read on, suddenly taking in every word at a cellular level. Studying his description of Gustave's hard hands on Bambi's soft body, and wishing daddy would take these stories off the page and into our lives.

With every paragraph, I grew hotter, and wetter. The spicy scent of my pussy rose to meet my senses, and I licked my lips as much from the taboo fear of being discovered, as from arousal.

I slid a finger inside myself and held my breath, desperate to get through the story and get out of the study before daddy got home.

"I know you can read, Biscuit."

I screamed, hearing daddy's voice from the door of the study. There was no way I could disguise the fact I was reading his story, but I could hopefully hide the fact I was jilling off to it.

Before I turned to face him, I slid my hand out of my shorts. Only then did I cross my legs and spin the chair around.

Daddy was standing there, his big arms crossed over his broad chest. The chest with that leopard tattoo on it.

I knew for sure that my face was red. Hopefully he'd think it was because of his words, and not my actions.

"Wh–what, daddy?"

"I said, I know you can read."

"Yes...?" Obviously. That's what I was doing at his computer.

"There's no way you could have missed my note on the door. Yet here you are. Not just breaking my rules about privacy, but also my ban on electronics."

"But daddy—"

"The only butt around here is the one I'm about to warm with my hand."

My entire core tightened as I recalled his description of Bambi being punished. The idea that daddy would spank my ass awoke a fresh burst of arousal inside me, and I felt certain it showed on my face.

"Stand up, Biscuit."

God, if I stood, then my shorts would probably fall down. I couldn't let daddy see me like that. He'd see my naked pussy, and know exactly what I'd been doing.

"Biscuit. I won't warn you again."

I grimaced with the onset of sheer embarrassment, and kept my thighs clamped together as I stood.

"Step aside."

I obeyed, taking tiny steps so I could keep my shorts up.

Daddy stepped past me and sat where I'd been. I noticed he took a sharp breath in, and only then did I remember how my scent had filled the air as I'd rubbed myself.

He said nothing about it, giving me hope that he hadn't noticed, after all. He simply swiveled his chair back around and briefly read his story before closing it and shutting down the computer.

"So, Billie Biscuit. You've found out my little secret."

"N–no. I just…I was trying to find an article about, um…"

"Save it, sweetie." He swiveled back around to face me. "And assume the position."

"The position?"

He tapped his thighs and I tilted my head to the side in confusion. Like a puppy. "You want me to sit on your lap?"

"No, no, Biscuit."

I was both disappointed and relieved. Maybe I could get out of here before any more embarrassment hit me.

"No, I need you to lie across my legs. Face down."

"What?"

"You disobeyed me, and you need a consequence."

"Fine. Ground me. Take away my…oh…"

"That's right, Biscuit. I've already taken your phone and laptop, and the message clearly didn't get through. So…" He tapped his thighs again, harder this time. With a sound so crisp it was almost like a whip cracking.

"You can't expect me to—"

"Can, and do. *Now.*"

There was such a fierce heat in his voice with that last word that I jumped like I'd been electrocuted. I swore my mind was saying *run away*, and yet my traitorous feet inched me toward daddy.

He reached his hand out and I placed mine in it. With a soft touch, he guided me down until I was exactly where he said. Lying face down across his muscular thighs.

A little pea-sized part in the center of my brain was screaming at me to leave. That he was way out of line with this. But that little pea was drowning in a sea of desire.

My boobs were getting mashed against his legs, which wasn't exactly the worst feeling in the world. But it was more than I could handle at that moment, so I inched forward.

Unfortunately, that pulled my still-open shorts down a little, and the sharp hiss of daddy's breath told me my ass was now officially creeping out of them.

"Biscuit, pull those down for me."

"What?"

"A spanking's not a spanking unless it's bare-assed."

"But...I mean, you can't. I won't let you."

He leaned down and murmured to me, his deep voice reaching me like an animal growl. "I don't see how you can stop me, sweetheart."

"Please, daddy."

"You didn't seem to mind reading about the many ways Gustave disciplines young Bambi."

I swallowed hard. "Disciplines? I–I didn't read that far." I wasn't even sure why I was objecting so much. I'd actually fantasized about this very thing. Daddy putting his hands on me. Being rough.

Spanking my tender young ass.

He chuckled, the sound coming at me more as a body-wide vibration than anything audible. "Then it's time for you to see what you missed. Shorts. Down."

The sheer ferocity in his voice at that point cowed any further protest on my part. I hooked my shorts in my trembling fingers and pulled them down, baring my ass completely.

I clamped my eyes closed as if that would somehow relieve my feelings of embarrassment. This man had been in my life for so many years. He wasn't my blood father, but he'd played the role all through my teenage years so far.

In a way, he was playing that role now. The disciplinarian. Only *punishment* was clearly not the only thing on his mind. Not if that hard lump pressing into my side was anything to go by.

He hacked right through my little daydream then, landing a white-hot spank in the heart of my right butt cheek. The sharp pain sliced my voice away for a moment, and I held my breath.

When my voice returned, it was little more than a soft whining sound. Even I couldn't tell if it was purely the pain that caused it…or if the wet heat that sprang up between my thighs was the real culprit.

Daddy rubbed his palm over the hot spot he'd created, working the skin-deep heat through to my muscle.

"You have a most delightful ass, sweetheart."

"Thank you, daddy."

"That was actually what first inspired me to write you into my books."

He landed another blistering slap, this time on the other cheek. It seemed to come from nowhere, and was far more shocking for that.

I struggled for breath as the pain bloomed across my skin.

"What was that for?"

"Oh, come now, Biscuit. You didn't think we were done, surely?"

"N–no." I swallowed the lump in my throat and squeezed my eyes shut. "But you could have warned me."

"Sweetheart, I did." He rubbed the new hot spot, like he had with the first. "In writing."

I sighed, putting in as much of the drama queen vibe as I could. "I know I did the wrong thing, daddy. It won't happen again."

The moment hung heavy before me. I'd never fantasized about being spanked, until I read it in daddy's book. If I hadn't disobeyed him, I wouldn't be getting that punishment. But I also wouldn't be getting so fucking wet.

He surprised me by dragging my shorts lower, until they simply let go, and got caught up on my ankles.

Daddy tugged in a series of short breaths through his nose, then growled with hunger.

"Biscuit, you're a very bad girl."

"I know, daddy. I'm sorry."

"But you smell so fucking good."

He knifed his hand in between my tightly-clamped knees and moaned.

"Your skin is like velvet." He dragged his hand upward, tickling at every millimeter of my inner thighs, but gliding out before he reached my drenched pussy lips.

Instead, he trailed his fingertips up to my ass and made random patterns with them.

"And here…a beautiful red velvet. Just like the cake."

I felt him moving, though I was still too chicken to open my eyes. The next thing I felt was his hot breath on my bare bottom.

"Only this pretty ass is far more delicious than any cake."

As if to prove himself right, he sank his teeth into the

flesh of my butt, dragging all my senses to that one small patch.

I gasped with the beautiful cocktail of desire and pain that gushed through me. When daddy switched from teeth to tongue, I simply moaned with want.

Again, though, he switched gears in an instant, taking his mouth away and replacing it with his hand. At speed.

He landed at least a dozen smacks on my ass, from side to side, from top to bottom. Every inch of my poor derriere got attention from his hard hands. And every impact pushed a higher, louder squeal from my throat.

"Please, daddy…"

"Yes, sweetheart?" he asked, his breath pumping that little bit harder. Whether that was just from effort, or from his own arousal, I couldn't tell.

"I've learned my lesson. Please…let me make it up to you?"

He stayed silent for a moment, apart from his breathing. Breathing which soon turned to growling.

"And just what do you think you can offer to appease me, Biscuit?"

"M–me?"

Daddy squeezed my ass and growled. "Oh, I'm already getting you, sweetheart. That's a foregone conclusion."

I swallowed hard, and then an idea came to me. "Then I can offer you inspiration."

"I'm listening."

"For more stories. I'll be your real-life Bambi. And you can get all the details right."

He trickled his long fingers down from my ass to my knees again, then sliced back up. Just like he did before. Only this time, he didn't pull out.

When he pressed his fingers to the slick heat of my pussy, I whimpered with shocked delight.

"That sounds perfect, Biscuit."

He ran the tips of his fingers up and down my wet lips, then took my clit between his finger and thumb, squeezing hard enough to send a pulse of electricity through my body.

I'd had my own fingers down there plenty of times. And I knew what felt good. But it had never felt as good as it did right then. Daddy had the magic touch.

Every tiny movement he made, every little change in pressure, awoke a new level of lust inside me. I hooked one arm around daddy's leg, holding on as if it could stop me melting to the floor.

I eased my thighs apart, without being asked to. I couldn't even be sure my brain had any control over the movement. It was as if they simply spread of their own accord.

Daddy growled even more raggedly than before, and eased the tip of one finger into my opening.

"Billie, you're a very bad girl."

"Yes, daddy. But please be gentle. I'm...I haven't..."

"Ah, fuck. You're a virgin?"

I squeezed my eyes shut, trying to hold in my tears of embarrassment. "Y–yes."

It was only a moment before he'd be laughing his head off and sending me away. What could a girl with no experience offer a man like him?

"That's fucking perfect." His voice still had that rough edge to it, but now it was coated in silk. "Just like Bambi."

Daddy curled one strong hand around my hip, and slowly spun his chair on the spot. I only realized we'd come around to face his desk when he pushed his keyboard aside. Straight down onto the floor.

"Up."

He barked the word out so sharply I almost missed it. When he dug his fingers into the skin of my inner thigh, I got the message quickly enough, and came up onto my feet.

Daddy patted the desk, where the keyboard had been only second before. "Here."

I stepped out of my shorts and planted my ass on the edge of his desk. Daddy turned his laser focus to my bare pussy and furrowed his brow.

"God damn, Biscuit. That is the fucking prettiest cunt I've ever seen."

Daddy had never used that word before. At least, not in front of me, and definitely not *to* me. I'd never liked the word before. But hearing the need in his deep, ragged voice, and seeing the hunger in his dark eyes, suddenly made it the most seductive word on the planet.

He eased his chair forward, and gently lifted my feet from the floor, one at a time. As he placed them down on his chair, either side of his legs, he closed his eyes and hauled in a long breath.

"You smell as beautiful as you look, sweetheart."

"Thank you, daddy."

He shocked me then by diving at me, landing his mouth right in the wet heart of my slit. He explored every inch of my hairless pussy with his tongue, from my navel down to my ass. He wet my upper thighs with spit and growled with the most intensely animalistic sound I could imagine.

A moment later, he pulled his head up as if surfacing from a long underwater dive. His eyes spun a little as he searched for me, sitting only a foot in front of him.

"Fucking hell, Biscuit. You look incredible, and you smell even better. But you taste like heaven."

"Ohh..."

He disappeared from view immediately, falling back down to devour me. Every swipe and jab of his tongue drove me higher, sending tingles of want up and down my spine.

Fearing I'd fall back and break his monitor, I swept my

hands into his hair and held on. His hot tongue, circling deep inside me, sent fresh waves of my scent gushing out.

The heat of his breath washed over my lips as he moaned and snarled his desire out against my tender skin. He had me nearly there, about to climax, with nothing but the power of his mouth.

Then, when he took my clit in his teeth and squeezed, I screamed out with desire as my orgasm steamrolled me into submission.

Pulse after hot pulse of pleasure filled me and subsided, like a heart beating. My entire body sparked with so much electricity I wondered if I'd somehow short out his computer.

Barely had the last spasm washed through me, when daddy stood and worked his belt open. Oh, god…I was finally going to see it. The only cock I'd ever wanted.

My hands trembled as I reached across, glancing up to meet his eyes. "M-may I, daddy?"

He curled his mouth up at the side and gave me a curt nod. "You may."

I fumbled the buttons of his jeans open, then held my breath as I pulled down, taking jeans and underwear in the one move.

It was already clear to me just how big and hard daddy was. But when I freed his cock, it leapt at my face like an angry serpent. I actually flinched as it bounced up, finally loose from its prison.

I wanted all of it, all at once. To touch his cock, and devour it, and have it inside me, everywhere it could go. As much as I'd always desired him, the sight of his thick cock sent me loopy. Seeing it there, stretching out from his body, all hard and hungry just for me…it was sheer perfection.

"Touch him." His voice had a tightness I'd never heard

before, and my pussy flooded again at the idea that I was the cause.

His dark, masculine scent drove in through my nose and snatched my mind from me. It was like a magic potion, and I was completely under his control.

I couldn't remember telling my hands to move. They simply rose from somewhere down below, and curled around his hot beast.

Daddy took a quick, slicing breath as I squeezed his shaft, and he rested one hand on my head.

"Kiss him, Biscuit."

For a second, I simply froze. I'd fantasized about this for maybe three years now. But what if I was useless at it? Would daddy simply laugh at me?

"Now."

The bark of that single word, so sharp and hot, sheared through my hesitation and had me jumping like I'd sat on an ant's nest.

My whole body trembled as I leaned in and pressed my lips to the fierce, hard heat of daddy's cock. Up close like that, his delicious musk seemed to prickle against my skin.

"Lick him."

I closed my eyes and parted my lips, pressing just the tip of my tongue to his skin. The salty flavor of him flooded my taste buds and a tiny whimper escaped my throat.

Slowly, I drew my tongue up his length, until I found the fat head on top. A small bud of clear fluid had peeked out the top and I flicked at it, drawing it into my mouth.

"Put it in, Biscuit."

Daddy's voice was little more than a gruff whisper, and I glanced up at him. There was a war taking place inside him. I could see it on his handsome face.

"What's wrong, daddy?"

He panted, in and out, a flurry of hard breaths. When he

found his voice again, it seemed to come up from halfway to hell.

"This." He slid his hand down to the side of my head, brought the other one up to stroke my cheek. "Every single fucking thing about what we're doing. It's so wrong, it's perfect."

"Perfect…" I let the word slide off my tongue like syrup. That was how I would have described it, too.

But daddy cut straight through the moment, making a gnarled fist in my hair and pulling it so hard I almost time-traveled.

"Are you still with me, Biscuit?"

"Ow! Yes, daddy."

"Put my cock in your mouth, please."

My jaw practically vibrated as I opened wide and angled his long shaft lower. I slid his mushroom head inside and closed, and his voice rolled out as a low growl.

"Good girl."

I'd seen enough porn to know the basics of blowjobs. Put it in, move your head up and down. But was that all? I wanted to do this the best I possibly could.

I slid my mouth lower, making little waves with my tongue against the belly of his cock. Daddy blew out a hard breath and relaxed his fist a little.

"Cup my balls, sweetheart."

That scared the hell out of me. What if I hurt him? But why would he tell me to do it if it was going to hurt?

I wrapped one hand around his thick cock and held his sac in the other. He moaned as I worked him, lifting those heavy balls and squeezing his shaft while I flicked at him with my tongue.

"Damn, Biscuit. You're a natural."

He scooped my hair up into a high, ragged ponytail, then took hold with both hands. As I bobbed up and down on him, he twisted his grip, pulling ever tighter on my poor, tortured scalp.

It hurt like hell. But that didn't matter, because it flooded my body with sparkling droplets of sheer delight. Droplets that formed a hot pool between my legs.

As daddy reacted to my mouth and my hands, he changed his grip, and the tension in my hair. In seconds, I understood how to read him. How to know whether what I was doing was right or wrong.

Following his unspoken directions, I grew bolder, and hungrier, sliding his length as far in as I could. Then coming back off him and lapping him from balls to tip, from left to right.

His deep moans grew drier, and tighter, and when I drove his cock back inside me, he made fists that turned my hair to lightning, firing blissful pain straight into my bloodstream.

The agony of my ecstasy was too much to bear, and I opened wide to let my moans free. As I released him, he drew his hips back and speared his hands down under my arms, lifting me bodily as if I were a doll.

He pulled me against himself, taking my mouth in a kiss that was years in the making. He completely subjugated my tongue, and I had no doubt at that moment that daddy *owned* me. Heart, soul and body.

Instinctively, I threw my legs around his waist, clutching myself to him as if I were scared he'd toss me away. He slid his hands down from my back, and cupped my naked ass, squeezing my flesh so hard the skin burned.

Daddy pulled free of my mouth and sank his teeth into the side of my neck. Through his soft mouthful he growled out his desires.

"You don't know how much I want this, Biscuit."

"Me too, daddy. I've wanted you forever."

He spun on the spot and my head went giddy as if I'd been drinking.

That's when I noticed the fat head of his cock. And exactly where it was pressing.

"Ohh…"

"You're my sweetheart, Biscuit. And I'm about to claim you."

"Yes, daddy. Please."

He stepped back, finding his chair and easing down into it. I could barely believe how easily he moved. Like I was no heavier than a kitten.

The moment he sat, I felt the pressure of his broad, fleshy tip in the slick mouth of my cunt. Even though I'd known this was about to happen, I was still completely unprepared. But more than anything, I wanted this.

Daddy pressed his lips to mine again, maybe just for distraction. I wasn't complaining. I'd been kissed by precisely six boys before this. And not one of them had anything like the power, the presence, or the skill that daddy had.

As my big man glided his thick tongue into my mouth, he shifted his grip on my ass. With an aching slowness, he lowered me, easing his long cock inside my pussy.

Every inch was like an eternity. The pain of him stretching me washed up against the bliss of him penetrating me. I whimpered with the sheer deluge of sensations as he filled my cunt, far beyond anything I thought I could take.

And then, I was sitting flat on daddy's lap. I had him—all of him—inside me. He still had his mouth pressed to mine, and his low growls of need vibrated against my lips.

I finally broke our kiss and leaned down, taking his ear between my teeth. "Oh, daddy…that's so fucking perfect."

"Hm. Almost."

"Daddy?"

He slid his hands up from my ass and onto my hips, stopping just to give them a hard squeeze. Then he put his weight against me, until I leaned back onto his desk. He took hold of my blouse and simply tore it open, my buttons flying like drunken bullets.

Daddy froze for a moment as he studied my bare breasts. My shock at being so roughly stripped eased quickly into excitement. The look on his face was one of rapture, and I knew it was my body taking him there.

"Sweet little Biscuit, your body is nirvana."

"Thank you, daddy."

He took my breast in one hand and seized my hip with the other. As he pumped me forward and back on his cock, he squeezed my lush tit and growled with want.

The stinging stretch in my pussy had eased to a beautiful aching heat, and every glide of his big cock in and out of me sent me spiraling further and further into some kind of pretty madness.

My words disappeared as my moans took over, and I fell back harder against the desktop, bending over backwards to please my man.

"Oh, fuck…" Daddy's voice turned hot and wet, and he glided his hand in from my hip to stroke my belly.

With my head hanging back, almost touching the desk, I couldn't see him, so I glanced into the mirror on the wall. With my back so fiercely arched, it put my tits up on display, and made them look even bigger than usual. But what seemed to be more interesting to daddy was how round my belly looked.

He had such a hungry expression on his face. One of ownership, of sheer possession. He explored my big breasts with his hard hands, and stroked my belly all over.

"You're going to be so fucking beautiful when you're pregnant, Biscuit."

"Ohh…thank you, dad—wait, what?"

"You're so luscious, sweetheart. So fucking fertile."

"But…"

"I want you, Biscuit, and I'm going to have you. You're mine forever."

The thought of being his, of being completely possessed by this man, was my fantasy come true. His strength lifted me. His praise made me whole.

But having a baby? I'd barely stopped *being* one. How could I have the slightest clue what to do?

Daddy pushed through my doubts. "I loved raising you, Biscuit, but I've always wanted a baby of my own. What better way to make you mine than to mark you?"

"M–mark me?"

He glided his hand up to the back of my neck, raising my head so he could look me in the eye. "You're a goddess already, sweetheart. But when you're with child, you'll blossom like you'd never believe. Here…"

Daddy cupped my breast, and leaned down to take my nipple in the heat of his mouth. He sucked gently, awakening a new level of want within me. Then he drove his teeth into the hard little bud and brought me back to the here and now.

"…and here." He pressed his hot palm to my belly and squeezed, gliding his thumb lower, creeping that hand down until he could press my clit.

"Daddy…" It was little more than a needy whine. Because I was already so close to climax, and now he was painting pictures of a future. Of a desire that transcended mere lust.

I'd always got a vibe from daddy that he was fond of me. I'd never allowed myself to believe he could want me the way I wanted him.

"My sweet girl, your belly will bloom with life. And your other little bloom down here?" He thumbed my clit and I yelped like a puppy. "She will be more beautiful than ever."

"Oh, daddy…"

He pulled me forward, slamming his mouth onto mine again. Every swab of his hot tongue, and every grind of his hard hips, drove me closer and closer to orgasm.

And then, at the thought of us truly coming together, and what it could mean—a baby—I felt a shift within me.

Daddy talked about how pregnancy would make me bloom. But just the idea of it, of making a baby with this man, had me blooming inside already. My heart swelled, my core begged, and more than anything, I needed him to fill me with his seed.

"Please, daddy," I murmured. "Give me your baby."

"Ah, fuck…"

He pulled me against him, grinding my tits against his chest as he squeezed my ass in both hands. He pumped me forward and back, and his rough hair scratched at my clit like a wild beast.

Seconds later, I felt a seismic shift in my belly, and I knew it meant only one thing. I was past the point of no return.

Daddy roared with ecstasy as he pumped deep inside me, the heat of his fluid filling my cunt. My own climax gushed through my body, meeting his in a tsunami of pleasure.

I clamped my mouth on his and kissed him like he was oxygen. Daddy groaned with need, kissing me back, and rolled us down off the chair. We landed on the floor, him on top of me, his hard cock still buried deep within me.

"Don't move, Biscuit. Let your body drink from me."

"Yes, daddy."

I curled my legs around his back and squeezed, as if milking every potent drop of his juice from inside him. Even so soon, I could feel it. He was taking root inside me.

Of course, I knew there was no way it could truly be happening, after only a minute or so. It was nothing more than a feeling. An instinct.

But I knew it, at a level that was beyond words. Even

words as powerful as daddy's. The words in his bad, bad books.

THE END
Get Access to over 20 more FREE Erotica Downloads at Shameless Book Deals

SHAMELESS BOOK DEALS is a website that shamelessly brings you the very best erotica at the best prices from the best authors to your inbox every day. Sign up to our newsletter to get access to the daily deals and the Shameless Free Story Archive!

SHAMELESS BOOK DEALS

The best place to get erotica recommendations tailored to you! Sign up for the newsletter below and find out why it's so good to be shameless! Free stories for subscribers.

Newsletter Sign Up

MORE FROM SHAMELESS
BOOK PRESS

Pseudo-Incest

Anything for the Man of the House (Ten Brats Who Learn How to Behave): These brats can pout all they want, they are going to do anything for the man of the house, even if what he demands is to take them hard and most certainly without using protection or pulling out. These stories are totally taboo and will leave you panting!

Pseudo-Incest

Submit to the Man of the House (Ten Brats who Give him Anything he Wants): The **brats** in these stories are about to give up their most carefully guarded treasures for flaunting those perfect little **fertile** bodies in front of the **men of their houses**. When these men decide that it's time for the little princesses to give them an **heir**, it's going to happen just the way they like it. **Hard, unprotected and all night long** even if it is the brat's **first time**.

Pseudo-Incest

Satisfy the Man of the House (Ten Brats who Give him Anything he Wants): These brats can pout all they want, they are going to satisfy the man of the house, even if what he demands is to take them hard and most certainly without using protection or pulling out. These stories are totally taboo and will leave you panting!

Gangbang/Menage

Taken 54 Times (54 Men. 10 Women. You Do The Math): How many could you handle? Two? Three? A dozen muscular athletes? How about trying all fifty-four? The women in these ten stories are taken hard every which way and just when they think it's over, there's another man who is just beginning. They are left messy, panting and oh so satisfied!

Pseudo-Incest

Owned by the Man of the House (Ten Brats who Learn how to Please Him): The man of the house lays claim to everything *in* his house, and that includes these precious little brats who think that they can get away with flaunting their perfect fertile bodies in front of him. When he decides to take what is his, he's going to take his pleasure **hard, unprotected and all night long**. They'll find how difficult it is to maintain a princess-pout when they're screaming his name.

MORE FROM SHAMELESS BOOK PRESS | 201

∼

Light BDSM
Shameless Submission (Ten Perfect Princesses Bend to his Will): True Masters come from all walks of life, some of them are the very pillars of our society, some of them are in our own homes. What they all have in common is that when they choose you as their submissive, you're left writhing in ecstasy, bent to their will, and life will never be the same again.

∼

Pseudo-Incest
Ravished by the Man of the House (Ten Brats who Learn How to Please Him): Those perfect pouts have been getting these little princesses everything they wanted for years. Now, for the first time, all they're getting is into the best kind of trouble with the Man of the House. They are going to be left a sweaty mess, legs quivering too hard to stand, and full of his special gift.

∼

E-Rom
Just Because You Love Me (Ten Bite-Size Spicy Love Stories): These stories go to show that just because you're in love doesn't mean you can't get it **hard**, it simply means you also get to cuddle afterwards. The women in this set are left with quivering legs, but whether that's because of the magic words or because of more... physical means is hard to decide!

∼

Pseudo-Incest

<u>Pounded by the Man of the House (Ten Untouched Princesses Who Learn How To Please Him)</u>: These beautiful brats may have fantasies of their virginity being taken by gentle lovemaking on their wedding night… but those are all pounded away as the men of their houses teach them how to really please a man.

~

Dubious Consent

TAKING Advantage (Ten Perfect Princesses Overwhelmed by Him): Their beauty has allowed them to take so much from this world. Doors are opened for them, favors are granted, gifts are given. Now it's time for these princesses to be overwhelmed, taken advantage of and have their legs opened for a very insistent gift that won't take no for an answer…

~

Pseudo-Incest

LUSTING for the Man of the House (Ten Untouched Princess Who Get What He Wants): These sexy brats have an itch that only the man of the house can scratch. They can't hold themselves back any longer, they *need* to give everything to the one man who makes them so wet they can't think straight.

***

Anal

The Tradesman's Entrance (Ten New Housewives who let Him in the Back Door): These sexy young housewives thought being a kept woman would be a dream come true, but while their husbands are away, they still have... needs. When the tradesmen come knocking these housewives fall under the spell of those rippling muscles. When rough hands bend them over, they only fight back a little, they need to give him what he wants... something nobody has ever taken from them before...

∼

Dubious Consent

TAKING Advantage 2 (Ten Perfect Princesses Overwhelmed by Him): Ten more untouchable princesses learn who is in charge. Taken, used, utterly betrayed by their own bodies they are victims of their own lust no matter how much they deny it.

∼

Pseudo-Incest

BROKEN in by the Man of the House (Ten Untouched Princess Who Get What He Wants): The man of the house is laying claim to all the fertile brats in his house. Even though it's SO WRONG, these untouched princesses are going to take what he gives them and love every dirty second of it.

Printed in the USA
CPSIA information can be obtained
at www.ICGtesting.com
LVHW052311290823
756688LV00020BA/278